"I want to thank you."

J.D. rode up beside her as she neared the corral. "You did a great job today with the herd."

Rachel avoided his gaze. "You're welcome." Her legs hurt so much she doubted she could get off her horse. She was unaware of the tears rolling down her cheeks. But he saw them.

"Damn. I knew I was asking too much of you. Come on, honey, slide into my arms. I won't let you go."

His gentle tones persuaded her as much as his strong arms, and she gave herself over to him.

"It's all right," he said, his voice husky with emotion. He held her even closer as he carried her to the house.

She laid her head on his shoulder, a sigh of contentment escaping her lips. She was in a miserable state, so why did she feel as if she'd died and gone to heaven? Because being in J.D.'s arms was all she'd wanted. For days. For months. But it wasn't enough....

Dear Reader,

I hope you will enjoy *Rachel's Cowboy*, my second book
in the CHILDREN OF TEXAS series. As the title implies,
I'm returning to my favorite type of hero—the cowboy. I
have to admit that I'm hopelessly drawn to them, especially
Texas cowboys! And so is Rachel Barlow, the stylish heroine
of this story.

My sweet spot for cowboys notwithstanding, the theme of
this series is family. It is a theme that occurs in many of my
books, because I think family is very important in all our
lives. Whether it is the traditional family, or a family made
up of friends or co-workers, it is the support and love one
receives from family that enables each of us to face the
world and conquer our fears.

In this book Rachel has lost confidence in her adoptive
mother and is alone in the world until she finds her birth
sisters, Vanessa and Rebecca. But she expands her new
family to include others, too. And of course, in the end,
Rachel finds true happiness and is ready to start a family
of her own.

I hope you'll come along for the ride as Rachel, Rebecca
and Vanessa discover other Barlow family members. And I
hope you celebrate your family every day for the warmth
and joy and support they give you.

If you have questions or comments, you can reach me at my
Web site, www.judychristenberry.com.

Judy Christenberry

Judy Christenberry

RACHEL'S COWBOY

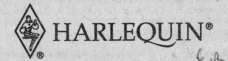

HARLEQUIN®

TORONTO • NEW YORK • LONDON
AMSTERDAM • PARIS • SYDNEY • HAMBURG
STOCKHOLM • ATHENS • TOKYO • MILAN • MADRID
PRAGUE • WARSAW • BUDAPEST • AUCKLAND

wW

ISBN 0-373-75062-5

RACHEL'S COWBOY

www.eHarlequin.com

Printed in U.S.A.

ABOUT THE AUTHOR

Judy Christenberry has been writing romances for over fifteen years because she loves happy endings as much as her readers do. A former French teacher, Judy now devotes herself to writing full-time. She hopes readers have as much fun with her stories as she does. She spends her spare time reading, watching her favorite sports teams and keeping track of her two daughters. Judy lives in Texas.

Books by Judy Christenberry

HARLEQUIN AMERICAN ROMANCE

HARLEQUIN INTRIGUE

*Brides for Brothers
†Tots for Texans
**Children of Texas

Don't miss any of our special offers. Write to us at the following address for information on our newest releases.

Harlequin Reader Service
U.S.: 3010 Walden Ave., P.O. Box 1325, Buffalo, NY 14269
Canadian: P.O. Box 609, Fort Erie, Ont. L2A 5X3

Chapter One

For the first time in her life, Rachel Barlow had time on her hands.

After working nonstop for the last six months, she stood in Vivian and Will Greenfield's spacious house, trying to rest. She didn't know how. Her constant worries and her hectic schedule had caused her to lose weight. Still, she couldn't stop fretting about her future.

Thanks to her adoptive mother, who'd stolen all of Rachel's savings and even borrowed money in Rachel's name, she'd been forced to take on one modeling assignment after another, with the hope of repaying the debt and building a nest egg. But in the process, she was about to crack.

Her two sisters—Vanessa Shaw, Vivian's adopted daughter, and Rebecca Jacobs, who was Rachel's twin—were concerned about her. They'd persuaded her to move into Vivian's home, where she could be taken care of.

Rachel looked around the lavish Highland Park home, which after six months she was still not used to.

Not only was it strange to be living in such luxury, so was having a loving family.

When the doorbell chimed, she called out, "I'll get it." Knowing the housekeeper would be in the kitchen, she figured she'd save Betty the trip.

She swung open the door and stared at the one man she'd never wanted to see again.

J.D. Stanley.

Frozen with horror, she said nothing.

Neither did he.

Then, when he took a step toward her, cowboy hat in hand, she asked, "What are *you* doing here?"

At the same time he demanded, "What are you doing *here?*"

Neither of them answered.

After another awkward silence, J.D. asked, "Is this still Vivian Greenfield's house?"

"Yes. Did you come to see her?"

He nodded.

"I'll get her housekeeper," Rachel said awkwardly, and backed away, leaving the door open.

She hurried to the kitchen. "Betty, J.D. Stanley is at the door. Do—do you know him? He wants to see Vivian."

"Why, sure, we know J.D. Tell him to come in," Betty said with a smile.

"I—I can't. I have to go upstairs." Rachel barely managed to blurt out the words before she scurried out of the kitchen and up the stairs, leaving Betty to welcome the guest.

Betty went to the door. "J.D., come in. Wait until I

tell Peter you've come." Her husband would be delighted to see the young man. She turned and headed for the kitchen, sure J.D. would follow. "I just put on a fresh pot of coffee. And I believe I have some chocolate-chip cookies left over. It's not easy keeping cookies around here. Joey, Rebecca's son, just loves them. And Peter, too."

She looked back and was surprised to find the man still standing on the doorstep. She retraced her steps. "J.D., what's wrong?"

"What's Rachel doing here?" he asked in a husky voice.

Betty looked at his unhappy face and then toward the stairs where she had disappeared. "Um, I think I'd better get Miz Vivian. You come into the library."

She took his arm and tugged him along, not leaving him a choice. "I'll get Peter to bring you something," she said once she'd seated him.

At the kitchen door, she told her husband what she wanted him to do. Then she hurried up the stairs.

RACHEL COULDN'T BELIEVE her luck. Lately it all seemed to be bad. No, that wasn't true. She'd found her real family, part of it at least, and that could never be considered bad. They were wonderful.

But they knew J.D.

She wanted to cry, but she didn't seem to have any tears left. Her…relationship, if you could call it that, with J.D. had happened right before she'd been bombarded with the devastation of betrayal and debt by her adoptive mother. The clothing designer who'd hired her had chosen J.D.'s West Texas ranch as the backdrop for a catalog shoot. She'd had the good fortune—or was it misfortune—of meeting J.D. then and spending a few days at his ranch.

In retrospect, her brief time with him had seemed such a betrayal. She hadn't trusted herself with anyone for a long time.

J.D. would take a break from his ranching chores occasionally and hang around the shoot. On her first day, she'd guessed it was curiosity that drew him. She'd noticed he held her hand longer than customary upon introduction, and his eyes had lingered on her throughout the day. On the second day, he'd become her shadow, showing up wherever she was. He took her on a long walk and he'd charmed her with his smile and wit, his manliness and his down-home courtesy. But there'd been more than that—an attraction she couldn't explain. On the third day of her stay, she'd submitted to the temptation that had been burgeoning between them, and fell into his arms in a stolen moment behind the barn.

She'd intended it to be just a kiss. Or two or three. But they'd ended up in his bed. J.D. had made the most exquisite love to her all through the night. His caress was gentle, but his possession of her left no doubt about how much he desired her. She'd fallen asleep on his shoulder, feeling safe and loved for the first time in as far back as she could remember.

She'd woken up alone.

He'd left to tend to his cattle, she'd surmised, knowing his daily routine. He'd left behind no note, no promise, no future.

With no reason to stay, and hiding her tears, she'd left promptly with the other models. But she hadn't forgotten that brief touch of heaven. And the betrayal that had broken her heart.

Now, finding him on the doorstep as she had, Rachel was devastated all over again. With a groan, she buried her face in her arms.

She had to pull herself together.

WITH A QUICK RAP on the bedroom door, Betty entered. Vivian, now six months pregnant, was resting on a chaise longue, reading a book.

"Miz Vivian, we've got problems."

The woman sat up and put her feet on the ground. "What's wrong?"

"J.D.'s here."

"Well, my goodness, Betty, that's not a problem. I knew he was coming sometime soon. I'll just go down and—"

"Miz Rachel opened the door. She knows him. When I told her to ask him in, she freaked out, said she couldn't, and ran upstairs."

Vivian came to an abrupt stop. "She knows J.D.? How? Maybe she thinks he's someone else."

Betty shook her head. "He knows her, too. He wanted to know what Rachel was doing here."

"Oh, my." Vivian couldn't think what was going on. True, Rachel hadn't been part of the family for long, but Vivian thought she was feeling more at home lately. "Go take him something to eat and tell him I'll be right down."

Once Betty had left the room, Vivian did what she always did these days when there was a problem: she called her husband. Will, a private investigator, always seemed to have the answer to whatever troubled her. They'd been married for almost a year now.

She dialed the number of his office. His assistant answered. "Carrie, it's Vivian. Is Will in?"

"Yes, ma'am. I'll put you through."

As soon as she heard Will's deep voice on the line, Vivian felt more at peace. "Dear, I think I need you to come home if you can."

Bless his heart, he never questioned her need of him. He merely said, "Okay" and hung up the phone, and she knew he'd be there within five minutes.

Drawing a deep breath, she headed for Rachel's room. If Vanessa or Rebecca had been there, she would've enlisted their help. But her daughter was at school, and Rebecca probably on her way to work.

Last year when she'd begun the search for Vanessa's five siblings, all of whom had been orphaned when their parents were killed in a car crash over twenty years ago, she'd only dreamed she'd be surrounded by the Barlow children. Rebecca had been the first of the Barlow siblings to be found, followed by Rachel. Vivian smiled when she thought of the beautiful reunion of the three sisters, and of the family that filled her house now.

She knocked on Rachel's door.

No answer.

Vivian opened the door a tad to find Rachel sprawled across the bed, her face covered by her arms. "Dearest, what's wrong? Was J.D. rude to you?"

Rachel immediately sat up and looked at her. "You know him?"

"Well, yes, of course. He manages my husband's ranch."

"I didn't know Will had a ranch."

"No, I meant my first husband, Herbert. He bought it years ago."

"Oh. I thought— Never mind. I just, uh, have a headache. I'm sorry if I was rude to him. Please apologize to him for me. I'm having a bad day."

"Of course, dear. Do you want Betty to bring you some headache medicine?"

Rachel grasped at that straw quickly. "Oh, yes, please, that would be wonderful."

Vivian backed out of her room and returned to her own. She called Rebecca at her husband's law office, where she worked in the afternoons.

"Hi, Viv. What's going on?" Rebecca asked as she answered the phone.

"It's Rachel. Could you come here and talk to her?" Since Rebecca and Jeff married five months ago and she'd moved into his home, Will and Vivian didn't see her as often as they used to.

"Of course. What's happened?"

"Well, I'm not sure, really. J.D. Stanley, who manages the ranch for us, came to the house and Rachel got upset."

"I'll be right there," Rebecca promised, and hung up the phone.

Vivian started downstairs. They were all worried about Rachel. As a fashion model for print ads, she didn't make the big bucks runway models made. Shortly before Rachel found Rebecca, she'd discovered that her adoptive mother, who also acted as her business manager, had been stealing Rachel's money ever since she started modeling at the age of fifteen. Rachel was left with almost nothing and owed a number of people from whom her mother had borrowed more money in Rachel's name.

Trying to pay her mother's debts and build up some savings again, Rachel had taken on more modeling jobs, which she'd come to hate. She'd lost weight, which she couldn't afford to do, and grown pale. Though it gave her an exotic look the cameras loved, everyone worried about her health.

Much to Vivian's relief, Will was coming in the front door when she reached the ground level. He rushed to take her in his arms, wanting to know what was wrong.

"I'm sorry, dear. I should've said the baby and I are fine." Vivian's first pregnancy at the age of forty-three had the entire household hovering over her, her husband most of all.

"Thank God!" Will whispered, holding her tightly. "So what's wrong?"

"J.D.'s here." Vivian gave Will the full explanation. "Rachel says she has a headache, but I think it's something more."

"Maybe she mistook him for someone else."

"He asked Betty what Rachel was doing here."

"Oh. So much for that theory." Will stepped away from her. "Well, want to come introduce me?" he asked, holding out his hand.

"Yes, thank you, Will."

When they reached the library, Peter was standing by the sofa, talking to J.D., who'd taken a seat. He immediately stood as Vivian and Will entered.

"Hi, Vivian," he said, a smile on his lips.

If Vivian hadn't known he'd been through an awkward meeting, she would think he was his normal calm self. She kissed him on the cheek and pulled Will forward. "J.D., this is my husband, Will Greenfield. Will, this is J.D. Stanley, our ranch manager."

The two men shook hands and they all sat down.

Betty came in with a plate of warm cookies. "Coffee for you, Mr. Will?" she asked, putting a glass of juice in front of Vivian. The doctor had taken her off coffee long ago.

"Yes, please, Betty," Will agreed.

"Betty, could you also take some pain reliever up to Rachel?" Vivian asked, watching J.D. out of the corner of her eye.

A spasm of pain crossed his face, but he said nothing.

Peter followed Betty out of the room and silence fell.

Vivian cleared her throat. "As always, I'm delighted to see you, J.D., but there seems to be a problem between you and Rachel. I didn't know you knew each other."

He frowned. "I think I mentioned in one of my letters that I'd allowed a designer to use the ranch as a backdrop for a photo shoot. Rachel was one of the models."

"Of course, I remember now. What an amazing coincidence," Vivian exclaimed, still smiling.

J.D. said nothing else.

It was Will's turn to try to find an answer. "I gather you two had problems?"

J.D. shrugged. "I think we were both surprised to see each other today."

"Oh, yes. Rachel said to apologize to you," Vivian stated.

He nodded.

"Did you want to discuss the ranch?" Will finally asked.

"I wanted to ask Vivian if she'd thought any more about selling the ranch to me. Since my mother's death, I've figured up my financial assets and I think I can swing a good purchase price."

Vivian nodded. "And you deserve to buy the ranch. You've done a great job of managing it for the past ten years after your dad's death. Will and I have talked about it, and we both feel that if you can offer a good price, we should sell the ranch."

J.D., a handsome young man, well built and clean-cut, looked guilty, which bothered Vivian.

"Isn't that what you want?" she asked.

"Yes, ma'am. But…how do you know Rachel Morgan?"

"She's Rachel Barlow now," Will said. "And she's one of Vanessa's sisters."

J.D.'s heart stopped. Rachel had gotten married? "How—"

Will was quick to explain. "She took back her original name, Barlow, after she found out who her birth family was."

J.D. started to breathe again, relieved that she hadn't married. But he was still confused. "I thought Madge said you'd found one sibling, named Rebecca."

"How is Madge, by the way?" Vivian asked, naming the longtime housekeeper on the ranch.

"Good. So, you found a second sister?"

"Yes, Rachel is Rebecca's twin." She paused as she heard the front door open. Leaning toward the door to the library, she called, "Rebecca, is that you? Come in and meet J.D. Stanley."

Much to J.D.'s surprise, a double for Rachel walked into the room. Except for being obviously pregnant, Rebecca looked exactly like Rachel—tall and dark-haired. After introductions, she excused herself and went upstairs.

"Um, I'm not sure you'll want to sell me the ranch now, Vivian. I've made a mistake. In fact, I'll find you a new manager. Just give me a month or two and I'll have everything set up." J.D. stood, his hat in his hand, edging toward the door.

Vivian and Will exchanged a look. Then Vivian stood and excused herself, saying she wanted to check on Rachel. "Will you join us for dinner, J.D.?" she asked over her shoulder.

She'd left the room before he could turn down her offer.

"Sit down, J.D. I think we need to talk." Will waited until the young man had done as he'd asked. Then he leaned forward. "I'm going to assume whatever happened between you and Rachel is private, having nothing to do with the ranch."

J.D. swallowed. "Yes, sir."

"Is she the reason you said you didn't think Vivian would want to sell the ranch to you?"

"Yes, sir. If she's part of the family, Vivian won't want to have anything to do with me."

"Did you do something against the law?"

"No, sir."

"Well then, what kind of offer are you making?"

J.D. stumbled over the figure he had carefully worked out.

"That's a very nice offer. I'll go over it with Vivian, but in the end, the decision will be hers, you understand."

"Yes, sir. I didn't mean to upset Rachel. But she may feel I have…not done the right thing."

"Dinner at seven?" Will suggested mildly, as if J.D. hadn't spoken.

The young man seemed confused and worried. Finally, he said, "Okay. You can call me at the hotel if Vivian changes her mind."

Will nodded and smiled.

VIVIAN, after a brief knock, slipped into Rachel's room. Rebecca was sitting on the bed with her twin.

"Are you feeling better, Rachel?" Vivian asked.

"Yes, I'm fine. Thank you for sending Betty up with the painkiller. Did—did Mr. Stanley leave?"

"Yes. But he'll be back to join us for dinner, of course," Vivian said, watching Rachel closely.

Her face remained expressionless and all she uttered was "Oh."

"I haven't seen J.D. since last year," Vivian explained. "And he wants to discuss buying the ranch."

Rachel stared straight ahead, not commenting on what Vivian had said.

Rebecca patted her sister's arm and asked, "Isn't the ranch big? How can he—"

"His mother died last year. He inherited a great deal of money from investments his parents had made. His father managed our ranch for twenty-five years. After he died ten years ago, J.D. took over the job. It's been his home all his life. He was actually born there, you know. And it's been his dream to own the place."

"Are you going to sell it to him?" Rebecca asked.

"Probably. He's a fine young man."

Rachel flinched, but she didn't raise her head.

Vivian continued. "However, he did seem concerned about something he felt he'd done that wasn't quite… appropriate."

Rachel leaped from the bed, her arms wrapped tightly around herself, and hurried to the far corner of the room, where she stared out the window.

Vivian stepped closer to her. "Sweetheart, did J.D. do something to hurt you? Did he take advantage of you?"

Rachel shook her head, but she didn't face Vivian.

Rebecca put her arms around her twin. "Tell us what happened, honey. You'll feel better."

"I was attracted to him and we—we made love." She told them the whole sordid story. "It meant nothing to him. I called him a couple of weeks later, and he couldn't even remember who I was." She looked at

Vivian. "He did nothing wrong. Just acted like a typical man."

Rebecca hugged her again. "Must be something about us that we get used by men."

"Not you, Rebecca," Rachel assured her, giving her twin a hug. "You and Jeff are perfect together."

"We are now, but it took a few years."

Rebecca and Jeff had known each other years ago, had loved each other years ago, before Jeff's aunt and uncle had taken him back to Texas, leaving Rebecca with a broken heart and an unborn child. Only when she herself was brought to Highland Park, after having been located in Vivian's search, did she see him again. Though that was almost five years later, it didn't take them long to realize that they were still in love and together would make a great family for their son, Joey.

Rachel was happy for her sister, but couldn't stop the twinge that went through her. Would she be so lucky?

She shrugged her shoulders. "I can't claim youth as the reason I had such poor judgment. But I'll survive." She hugged Rebecca again. "At least I have you and Vanessa now."

Vivian added, "And me and Will, too."

"Yes, you and Will are remarkably generous people," Rachel agreed with a smile. "And I shouldn't have reacted as I did to one of your guests. I've been on edge for so long, and I felt safe here." She gasped and said hurriedly, "Of course I know J.D. wouldn't— It was just the shock. I'm sorry, Vivian. That's a terrible way to repay all you've done for me."

"Nonsense!" Vivian protested. "You haven't cost us

much of anything. You don't eat enough to keep a bird alive."

Rachel smiled, but it didn't have any humor in it.

"In fact," Rebecca said, catching her sister's hand, "we're all worried about you. You mustn't lose more weight, Rach. You're too skinny already."

"Haven't you heard you can never be too thin or too rich?" Rachel said, a teasing note in her voice.

But Rebecca wasn't amused.

"Look," Rachel said, squeezing her sister's hand, "I appreciate your concern. But right now I have to concentrate on my work." She smiled. "You know I always come back here between jobs."

"Of course. We want this to be your home, Rachel," Vivian insisted.

Rachel leaned forward and kissed her cheek. "Thank you."

"You will join us for dinner tonight, won't you? I don't want J.D. to think he's not welcome here, too."

"I could just—"

Rebecca squeezed her hand.

"Yes, of course, Vivian, if you want me to dine with J.D., I'll be glad to do so." Rachel looked at her twin for her nod of approval. She had grown hungry for that familial camaraderie that she'd never had in her life.

"Good. I'll see you both at dinner." Vivian slipped from the room, leaving the twins alone.

"I'm sorry, sis," Rebecca said softly. "I didn't know you knew J.D."

"I guess I don't. I'll admit at the time I thought I was slumming a little, sleeping with a cowboy. But there was something about him. Right after that is when I found you and discovered my mother had not only stolen all my money but had also put me deep into debt. That was a major distraction."

"Yes. I'm glad you took her name off all your accounts."

"I even feel guilty about that. I shouldn't have offered her such a temptation."

"Rach, you were fifteen! You didn't have a choice then."

"I know, but...I was careless with my life. I'll make it back and I'll be careful with the money I make now. I have to be. Modeling is all I know how to do."

The sadness in Rachel's words brought tears to Rebecca's eyes. "You have a lot of talent, Rachel. You're going to be all right."

"Yes, of course," Rachel agreed, but there was nothing convincing in her tone.

J.D. STANLEY PACED his hotel room, covering the twenty-odd feet in a few steps. He'd put on a suit for dinner with Vivian and her husband. He might be a cowboy, but he knew how to dress while in the city. No boots tonight.

He would've been excited about making a deal to buy the only home he'd ever known, if it weren't for Rachel. He hadn't expected to see her when the door had opened at Vivian's house earlier that day.

Seeing her there, framed in the carved oak doorway, was like watching a dream come to life. She'd been starring in his nighttime fantasies for months. He remembered how beautiful she'd looked when he made love to her, how her eyes had flared when he took possession of her.

Today her eyes flared again—but with a different emotion. Was it shock he saw in those blue orbs? Embarrassment? Regret? Or anger?

Or was it just the reflection of his own feelings? He'd spent the remainder of the day reining in those emotions, finding a measure of control. Now he was ready for her—as much as he could be ready for Rachel.

If she came to dinner tonight—and he doubted she would—he could greet her as a stranger. He was prepared.

As much as he'd loved being with Rachel, making love to her, he had to admit they had nothing in common. By the time he'd left her in his bed early that morning, he'd known he'd made a mistake. He started his day at six each morning, while she seldom rose before nine. He ate big meals to fuel his work. She ate carrot sticks for a treat. He wore jeans; she wore swimsuits in winter and fur coats in July. Since they'd known each other for only three days, he wasn't sure they had any similarities.

It made him feel that their whole relationship was shallow. So why had she haunted him for six months?

Something happened when their skin touched.

Her slender grace and those teasing blue eyes drew him. She laughed as if he were in on the joke, rather than laughing at him.

He'd gotten up at six the next morning, a little groggy, which made his job dangerous, and she'd packed and left with no note, nothing.

So she'd realized their unsuitability, too.

The first time she'd called, he'd been out with the cattle and she'd talked to Madge. She'd left no message. When she called that evening, the ranch had been enveloped in a brutal storm with raging winds that made reception sporadic at best. He could barely hear her, but he'd managed to ask the most important question. Was she pregnant? He had to know. He couldn't believe he hadn't taken precautions, but their passion had surprised him. He'd made a mistake.

Rachel had hung up the phone without a reply.

He'd heard nothing from her until today.

He grabbed his keys and walked out of the hotel room. He'd have to explain to Vivian what happened. Or maybe he could explain to Will. He liked him, and it would be easier to explain his indiscretion to a man.

J.D. wended his way through the tree-lined streets of Highland Park. The homes were stately, the landscaping perfectly manicured. Still, he couldn't imagine living in such enclosed neighborhoods, unable to ride his horse or to see into the distance. He'd bet Rachel fit right in, though.

He took a deep breath as he killed the engine. He was ready to go in. After all, the woman meant nothing to him. He hadn't done anything to her that she didn't want. Shaking his head as if to clear away the memories, he opened his truck door. He didn't need to be thinking about that night.

Peter opened the door in response to his knock. With a smile, he welcomed J.D. inside.

"Thanks, Peter. Are Vivian and her new husband waiting for me?"

"A'course they are. All the family is gathered in the family room. You know the way."

He did. Ten years ago, when his father had died of a heart attack, he'd come to tell Vivian and her husband, Herbert, that his dad was dead. And he'd had the nerve to apply for the job his father had handled—managing the ranch.

It had been Vivian who'd supported him in his request. Normally, she didn't argue with her husband. But when Herbert had said he'd look for someone with more experience, Vivian had insisted that that hardly seemed fair. She'd suggested J.D. be given the job on a temporary basis so he could prove his worth.

J.D. owed her a lot.

With a deep breath, he strode down the hall to face the "family."

Chapter Two

Rachel was almost sitting on her hands. A childhood habit of biting her nails when she was nervous seemed to be threatening her again.

Suddenly J.D. appeared in the doorway. He hesitated before he stepped into the room. Will stood and offered him his hand. "Come on in, J.D. We've been waiting for you."

"I'm sorry if I'm late," he immediately said, looking at Vivian.

"Of course you're not late, dear," she answered.

She would've said the same thing if he'd been an hour late, because she was a very forgiving lady. But he was actually on time. Rachel had found Vivian to be a wonderful hostess, always forgiving the worst social faux pas.

Rachel had never seen J.D. in city clothes. But she had to admit they didn't lessen his impact. In a taupe shirt and brown suit that matched his hair and eyes, he was a handsome man, with broad shoulders, slim hips and a determined look that said people shouldn't get in his way.

As she had.

Vanessa stood and gave him a hug. "Welcome back, J.D. It's been too long."

"It must've been, 'cause you're all grown up, Vanessa," he said with a warm smile. "I think you were sixteen the last time I saw you."

It hadn't occurred to Rachel that J.D. might be interested in Vanessa. But she was a beauty and had what Rachel no longer had—money. She said a silent prayer that Rebecca hadn't told Vanessa about her problem with J.D. She didn't want to have spoiling Vanessa's romance on her conscience.

J.D. then greeted Rebecca and Rachel, commenting on their similarity in looks.

He was lying, Rachel thought. She knew what her exhaustion and worry had done to her looks. She used to be able to appear in pictures wearing very little makeup. Now she spent more time on makeup and still looked wan.

Rebecca put her arm around Rachel. "It's so exciting to have my twin here. It's amazing how much we're alike."

J.D. nodded and smiled, but he didn't bother confirming the lie.

Vivian looked over his shoulder. "Are we ready, Betty?" she asked as the housekeeper appeared in the door.

"Yes, Miz Vivian. Don't want it to get cold."

They all walked to the dining room.

"Where's your son?" J.D. asked Rebecca. "Peter says he's a fine boy." He took the seat on Vivian's right. He was sharing that side of the table with Vanessa, leaving the other side to the twins.

"He prefers to eat with Betty and Peter. He doesn't get to see them as much since we moved in with Jeff after the wedding," Rebecca said.

"Unless our company includes Jeff," Will added. "It's impossible to keep those two apart."

Rebecca beamed at Will. "It's true. He and Jeff loved each other from the start."

"When did you get married?" J.D. asked.

"Last October, as soon as Jeff got *un*engaged to Chelsea. She immediately got engaged to his partner, and now we're all one big happy family."

J.D.'s sideways grin, which tugged on Rachel's heart, was his only answer, but there was obvious approval in it.

"Jeff would've joined us this evening, but he does volunteer work at the legal aid office on Thursday nights," Vivian said.

"Good man." J.D. nodded and accepted the bowl of fruit salad Vanessa was offering. "And how about you, Vanessa? Any boyfriends on the horizon?"

She gave him a flirtatious smile. "Only you, J.D."

"Then I'd say these city boys are a might slow!"

Vanessa giggled and Will and Vivian laughed.

"Oh, did Madge tell you our baby is a boy?" Vivian asked.

"No, she didn't. In fact, she didn't even remember to tell me you had remarried and were expecting until I got ready to leave. That was a lot to adjust to all at once. Congratulations."

"Thanks," Will said. "I think it was a lot for me and Vivian to adjust to, too, but we're very happy."

"I guess so. I haven't seen Vivian look so young in a number of years." J.D. smiled at his hostess.

Rachel tried to concentrate on her dinner plate and ignore the fire burning in her stomach. She couldn't possibly be jealous of Vivian, could she? But the warm smile J.D. had given Vivian was a long way from the brief nod she'd received.

Dinner progressed, with Rachel stirring around on her plate what little food she'd taken, seldom tasting anything. She feared she'd throw up and look like a fool. She was giving J.D. Stanley too much power over her life. What little life she had.

"Vivian says you're going to the Bahamas to shoot swimsuits. Won't it be a little chilly this early in the year?" J.D. asked, looking at Rachel directly for the first time.

She glanced up, shocked to realize he was speaking to her. "No. No, the Bahamas are always warm." She hoped. It might not be warm enough to swim, but she didn't intend to get wet. She wasn't going for fun.

As if he cared.

He didn't speak to her for the rest of the meal.

Afterward, Will, Vivian and J.D. went into the library to continue their business discussion.

Rachel breathed a sigh of relief. She looked up to realize Rebecca and Vanessa were staring at her. "What?"

"Are you okay?" Vanessa asked. "You hardly ate anything."

Rachel shrugged. "I have to wear a swimsuit." It was as good an excuse as any. "Vanessa, are you and J.D. close?"

Vanessa grinned. "Yeah, like brother and sister... who only see each other every five to ten years."

"He's very handsome," Rachel pointed out.

"Yes, he is, and he hardly realizes it, which is one of the best things about him. If you want him, go get him. I'll be on your side."

Rachel looked at her twin. "You didn't tell her?"

Rebecca shook her head. "I didn't know what you wanted."

Rachel swallowed. She wasn't used to such consideration. "I— J.D. and I have a p-past. I don't think there's anything left for us. But thanks, anyway."

"That's too bad," Vanessa said, frowning.

"I think I'll go on to bed. I need to be up early."

"You're leaving tomorrow?" Rebecca asked, surprised.

"Yes, but I'll be back next Thursday, so it won't be a long trip. I'll be gone in the morning before you get up," she told her sisters.

Rebecca spoke up. "Rachel, I'm worried about you." She looked at Vanessa. "We both are. Why can't you take some time off?"

"After all, Jeff managed to get back some of the money your mother stole from you," Vanessa added.

Rachel was touched by their concern, but she knew what she had to do. She leaned over and kissed them goodbye. "Take care while I'm gone, you two."

J.D. HAD HIS DREAM.

After a brief discussion Vivian agreed to sell him the ranch. She argued about the purchase price, thinking his offer too high rather than too low. He assured her he knew the value of the land. Besides, he pointed out, that wasn't the way to do business. Herbert would turn over in his grave.

"You're right—he would, J.D. But Herbert didn't understand what was important."

"I know, Vivian," J.D. agreed. "He wasn't nearly as smart as you."

Will laughed. "Well, it's good to see we're all in agreement."

J.D. felt his earlier tension seep away. He was among friends. "About Rachel… I didn't mean to take advantage of her. She came— I mean, she indicated her interest and we shared a few moments. But I didn't force her or anything."

"I never thought that, dear," Vivian assured him.

"And Rachel didn't say anything like that," Will added. "I think it was the surprise of seeing you suddenly in a place where she felt safe."

"Safe? What is threatening her?" J.D. demanded.

Vivian explained briefly about Rachel's mother.

"Damn!" J.D. hung his head. When he looked up, he said, "I didn't like that woman. She expected to be waited on hand and foot, and she did nothing. Madge just about threw her off the ranch."

"Yes." Vivian nodded, her strawberry-blond hair shimmering in the light. "That sounds like an accurate description. Rachel had found out about her adoption and Rebecca just after she'd discovered her debt. It was such a betrayal. I think she went into shock. We've tried to reassure her, but she's independent. And worried about her future."

J.D. stared at his hosts. "That's a hard knock."

"Yes, it is, but we're trying to help her. And Will is still looking for the one brother we haven't found. Just recently the girls received a letter from Jim, their oldest brother, but he won't be home for a few months yet."

Thinking of Rachel and what she'd been through, J.D. felt inundated by emotions he couldn't name—except for frustration. That one he could easily identify. Frustration because of how their time together had ended, frustration because there was no way to help her. Finally he changed the subject. "Now that we've agreed on the sale, what do we do?"

Vivian looked at Will.

"If you've got the money ready, then all we need is to get the papers ready. I think we can plan on closing next Friday. Will you go back to the ranch or stay here all week?"

"As long as it's all right with you two, I'll go back to the ranch and work. I'll return next Thursday so I'll be here on Friday for the closing, whatever time it is."

"That will be great," Will said, standing to shake his hand. Vivian gave him a kiss, and J.D. escaped from the house where Rachel was living.

It was time to get back to his real life.

A WEEK LATER, J.D. made the drive again to Dallas, this time to sign the papers that would make him owner of his home. There was excitement in him as he achieved a major goal. There was also an edginess that he would again have to face Rachel.

Maybe she wouldn't be back from the Bahamas. It would be a shock to come from warmth and sunshine to Dallas in March. A cold front had moved through this week, bringing rain, sleet and wind.

Before he went to the hotel, he wanted to stop by Vivian's house and let her know he was here. As he pulled up to the curb, he saw a taxi, but no one appeared to be in it. Then he saw two people who'd apparently exited it.

Rachel, as white as a sheet, must have just fainted. The taxi driver, a small man, was holding her, but seemed to be on the verge of dropping her. J.D. threw his truck into Park and darted up the sidewalk to help.

He took Rachel in his arms and told the driver to ring the bell. When Betty answered the door, she realized at once that Vivian was needed. She opened the door wide for J.D. to carry Rachel in.

"Take her to the morning room. I'll get Miz Vivian."

J.D. did as she asked. As he carried Rachel, he realized she was running a high fever. What the hell had they done to her in the Bahamas?

Vivian came down the stairs at a faster rate than she should have. She headed for Rachel as soon as she entered the room. J.D. stopped her. "Vivian, I don't know what's wrong, but I do know she's running a high fever. I think she needs to go to a hospital."

"Oh my, yes. I'll get my purse."

"I don't think you should go, Viv. It could harm the baby. I'll take her. Just tell me who to ask for."

Clearly frustrated, Vivian reluctantly gave J.D. her doctor's name. "I'll call him and ask him to meet you there."

"Good. Do you have a blanket we can wrap her in? It's not exactly warm out there."

"Oh, yes. Betty?" Vivian called. The housekeeper was hovering just outside the door. "Bring a blanket for Rachel."

J.D. wrapped her in the coverlet Betty brought and lifted her into his arms again. "Hell, she hardly weighs anything! A strong wind would carry her away."

"I know. She's so fragile," Vivian said tearfully. "You'll call as soon as you learn something?"

"Sure, Vivian. I'll call."

He returned to his truck, carrying Rachel. He laid her across the bench seat and got in after her. Then he put her head on his thigh and made the short drive to the hospital.

THREE HOURS LATER, Rebecca had finished her classes, skipped her job at Jeff's office and was at the hospital looking for her sister. She was directed to the second floor, where she found Rachel's room and hurried in, only to find J.D. Stanley sitting in a chair by her bed.

"J.D.? How is she?"

"She has pneumonia. It appears the weather there was unusually cold and wearing a swimsuit was risky."

"Has she come to?"

"A couple of times. She's not really clear about where she is or why." He shook his head and muttered, "She thinks she's invincible."

"But she'll get better?" Rebecca's voice was tight with worry.

He nodded. "Vivian's doctor, Dr. Clayburn, says it will be a long recovery. She's way too thin and weak."

"We'll take care of her," Rebecca said staunchly.

"What about you and Vivian?"

"What do you mean? We will want to take care of her."

J.D. hated to tell her what the doctor had said. "I don't think the doc wants Vivian or you to be around her. The babies might be affected. In addition to pneumonia, Rachel may have a viral infection." Rebecca wasn't as far along in her pregnancy as Vivian, but was still susceptible.

Rebecca paled. "Oh, no! I hadn't thought of that. What are we going to do?"

"I've got an idea, but I doubt that you'll like it," he said slowly, as if still considering it himself. "I'll talk to Will about it."

As if she felt the tension in the room, Rachel stirred.

"Rachel?" Rebecca asked softly.

"Becca? I'm so tired." She closed her eyes again.

"I know, sis. Just rest."

Before Rebecca finished speaking, Rachel was asleep again.

"They're giving her a strong antibiotic in the drip, and he added a sedative to conserve her energy. He's expecting her to sleep until tomorrow," J.D. said. "If you can get Vanessa to stay with her for a few hours, I'll go back to the house and discuss what's to be done with her."

Though she nodded, Rebecca seemed in shock. She looked so lost. J.D. reached out and gave her a brief hug. Finding your family didn't always mean things were easy, he thought.

He didn't want to leave Rachel, either. She was weak and had no idea what was happening to her. He was glad her sister Vanessa could stay with her for a while. When she arrived, J.D. headed to Vivian's.

Vivian joined him in the library, wanting to know how Rachel was.

J.D. filled her in on everything Dr. Clayburn had said. "They're hoping to get control of the fever by tomorrow."

"Good. Then we can bring her home?"

"No, Vivian. Dr. Clayburn doesn't want you or Rebecca around Rachel until she's completely well." J.D. already knew Vivian would protest. But he was counting on Will putting his foot down.

Vivian reacted as predicted. "That's ridiculous! He's an old woman! I'm sure it won't hurt the babies."

Will came in in time to ask questions. When he heard what the doctor had recommended, he agreed. Vivian immediately began to argue.

"I have a solution," J.D. said loudly, stopping the argument.

"You do?" Will asked eagerly.

"Yeah. There's plenty of peace and quiet on the ranch…and Madge was a nurse. Remember? She looked after Mom the past five years."

"That's right," Vivian said. "I'd forgotten that fact, because she's such a good housekeeper."

"You think about it, Vivian. I promise I'll keep my distance so Rachel will be comfortable."

"But we shouldn't ask you to give up your own comfort for our family," Vivian said.

"It won't affect me. I'm out working until dark. We're into the calving season."

Will offered his hand in a shake. "We'll discuss it. You'll be ready to sign the papers tomorrow?"

"Yes. That's why I stopped by, to let you know I was here and ready."

"Good timing," Will added.

Vivian hugged him in gratitude. "Come to dinner this evening, J.D. Will and I will discuss your generous offer and we'll talk again tonight."

It was all J.D. could ask for at this point. He said, "I'll be here at seven."

BEFORE HE RETURNED to Vivian's house, J.D. went to the hospital. He had a spare hour and told Vanessa to go grab a meal. She needed the break and he wanted to be alone with Rachel.

While she was sleeping, he could look his fill at the beauty who had haunted him for the past six months. He'd told himself she was just another woman, but he couldn't forget their night together.

He would have to avoid her if he took her home to Madge. He'd called his housekeeper when he got back to the hotel. She'd been thrilled with the idea of caring for Rachel. She'd liked Rachel, and she missed nursing. Madge had immediately begun planning healthy meals.

She'd also volunteered to call Vivian and reassure her that Rachel would receive the best care.

J.D. reached out and stroked Rachel's cheek. In spite of her illness, her skin was still soft. He was going to be in hell, having Rachel around but being unable to touch her. But he'd even suffer hell if it made her healthy again.

Chapter Three

J.D. stayed an extra day at the hotel, spending the night after they signed the papers. The doctor promised to release Rachel after she ate some breakfast the next morning.

J.D. had breakfast with Will and Vivian. Afterward, Betty made the back seat in his double-cab truck look like a bower of sleep for Cinderella, or maybe that was Sleeping Beauty. He got confused on those fairy tales.

At the hospital, the doctor gave him lengthy details on Rachel's care and questioned him about how he would get her to his ranch. Then he had him drive his truck to the door of the hospital, promising to have Rachel brought down in a wheelchair.

J.D. had hoped he'd be able to carry her out asleep. Vanessa assured him she'd explained the arrangements to Rachel, but J.D. figured if she was awake, she might refuse to get in his truck with him.

He saw her at once, slumped in her wheelchair in front of the hospital as he drove up. Scrambling from the truck, he hurried around to open the door for her. Then he faced Rachel.

"Betty fixed the back seat so you'll be comfortable," he assured her. "Shall I lift you into the truck?"

"I think that would be the only way I could get in," Rachel said in a whisper, glancing away. The nurse gave him a suspicious look. J.D. decided he'd better move quickly before the woman accused him of being an ax murderer.

He placed Rachel on the soft pillows Betty had put at one end so she was propped up a little, and wrapped the blankets around her. Immediately she closed her eyes and appeared to again be sleeping.

"You have all her medicines and the instructions the doctor gave you?" the nurse asked.

"Yes, I do. And she'll be under a nurse's care within three hours, I promise."

"Good. She should sleep at least that long. The doctor gave her a sedative so the trip wouldn't strain her."

"Good thinking. Thank you."

He closed the truck door and got in on the driver's side. Dallas was a nice place, as cities went, but he was ready to get back to the wide-open spaces of West Texas.

Once he was on the road, the traffic demanded most of his attention. He could glance back over his shoulder and barely see her face, snug in the covers. Once he got past Fort Worth, the traffic thinned out, and he picked up his pace. If she woke before he got her home, he wouldn't know what to do for her.

Thank God for Madge.

ONE WOULD'VE THOUGHT he'd rung an alarm when J.D. pulled up beside the house he'd been born and raised in. Before he could kill the engine, Madge came out of the house, followed by two cowboys carrying a stretcher between them.

"I've been so anxious for you to get here. How is she?" Madge asked, peering in at his own personal Sleeping Beauty.

"The doc gave her a pill to put her to sleep. I haven't heard a peep out of her. What's the stretcher for?"

"To get her in the house, of course."

"We don't need that. I can carry her." He was determined to hold her in his arms once more. He looked at the two cowboys. "Vivian packed her a couple of bags in the back. Can you grab those?" Then he said to Madge, "Do you have her bed ready?"

"Of course I do. The cover's even turned back, waiting for her." Madge was always ready, no matter what he asked of her.

J.D. slid his hand under the blankets, feeling Rachel's warmth through the soft flannel. "She may be running a fever."

"Wouldn't be surprised. It will be a couple of days before we get rid of the fever. Did you bring the antibiotic drips?"

"Yeah. They packed them on ice for me. They're in the back of the truck, too."

"I'll get one started right away. We still have that metal tree we used for your mother. I put it beside her bed."

He lowered Rachel to the bed after Madge had

peeled away the blankets from the truck, so Rachel would be comfortable while she slept. A sigh escaped her pale lips as she snuggled down under the coverlet, curling away from him.

Madge put a hand on his shoulder. "She's going to be fine, J.D. You did a good job getting her here. The boys need to talk to you about a problem that came up while you were gone. They're having coffee in the kitchen. You can leave Rachel to me."

He didn't want to. But he reminded himself of his promise to keep away from her. Right. He'd turn his thoughts to cows.

And later, when Madge had gone to bed, he'd check up on Rachel.

EVERY EVENING for the next few days, J.D. listened to Madge's account of Rachel's day, telling him what she'd eaten, how long she'd slept, what her temperature had been. Then, after Madge went to bed, J.D. would creep into Rachel's room and sit in the chair by the bed, watching her sleep. He'd tell himself that he hadn't thought about her all day, hadn't worried about her as he went about his ranching chores. But the truth was he found himself looking forward to Madge retiring to her room after puttering in the kitchen.

Was it right that he anticipated his visit with Rachel as much as he did?

The question nagged him every night, but he never answered it.

Occasionally, he'd even permit himself to touch her cheek, just briefly, to see that she wasn't too hot.

Until the night her eyes opened.

He jerked back, unable to look away. "Uh, I wanted to be sure you weren't running a fever."

To his surprise, she smiled wanly at him and closed her eyes again, as if he'd interrupted her dreams. After waiting a moment, he stood and tiptoed out of the room. The sight of her blue eyes went with him.

The next morning, Madge reported that she was going to get Rachel out of bed that day to sit for a while in the kitchen.

He looked at her sharply. "You don't think you're rushing things?"

"No, I don't. We've finished all the antibiotic packs and she hasn't run a fever for three days. She's getting bored and restless in bed. I think she'll do better for the variety."

"I could move my television into her room."

"That would be nice of you, J.D., but she's not going to stay in that bedroom all day. She's going to join me in the kitchen for lunch."

He frowned. "Is she eating real food?"

"What did you think I was feeding her?" Madge asked with a grin.

"Soup, I guess."

"No, she eats real food. Why?"

"I thought I'd have lunch in today. I'm going to be working close by. A warm meal and a good fire would keep me going in that cold wind this afternoon."

"Terrific. I'm sure she's tired of seeing only my old face all day long. Come in for lunch."

He really had planned on joining Madge for lunch before he heard about Rachel's getting out of bed. He told himself that over and over again. Then he got angry with himself. It was his house. He owned it now. He and the bank. If he wanted to come in for lunch, he could.

But at noontime he approached the house with trepidation. What if Rachel got upset at seeing his face? Madge would have some questions for him in that case. Using the facilities in the closed-in porch, he cleaned up before he came into the warmth of the kitchen.

"Oh, good, you're here," Madge said with a cheerful smile. "I told Rachel you'd carry her to the table so she could save her energy for eating."

"And she was okay with that?"

"Of course. She's waiting for you," Madge assured him as she bustled around the kitchen getting their meal ready.

J.D. rapped softly on the closed door of Rachel's room.

"Come in," she called.

He pushed open the door and found her sitting up in bed, her hair in a neat braid and lipstick on her full lips. She looked good, and suddenly the thought of holding her body against his was making him very nervous. He should have eaten with the men. "I'm here to carry you to lunch. Ready?" Not that he was anymore.

"Yes, thank you."

He started talking as he approached her, hoping to distract her from his nervousness. "You've improved a lot in one week, Rachel. I guess Madge knows what she's doing."

"Oh, yes, I think so." She shoved the covers back and slid her long legs over the side of the bed. She was wearing a pink nightgown and a matching robe that complemented her lipstick.

Staring straight ahead, he slid his hands under her legs and around her shoulders and lifted her against him. "But you still haven't gained much weight."

At his remark, Rachel turned to give him a look, and her mouth was mere inches from his, way too close for his comfort. He whipped his head straight as she said, "I've been eating as much as I can."

"Maybe I'll start you running laps around the house to build up your appetite."

"I wish I could," she whispered.

"Soon, Rachel, soon." He didn't add that when she got that well, she'd be heading back to Dallas and her sophisticated life. But he knew it was true.

When they reached the kitchen, regret and joy warred within him. He could finally walk away from the temptation of touching her, but his arms felt lonely when he put her in the chair Madge indicated Rachel should use, the one closest to the fireplace, where a cheery blaze was flickering. "We don't want you getting sick again, child."

J.D. took the seat next to her. Madge raised her eyebrows but said nothing. She started them off with bowls of homemade tomato soup.

Rachel took her first spoonful and looked up in surprise. "I didn't think I liked tomato soup, but this is delicious."

"Thank you, Rachel. It's my own special recipe."

Madge passed some slices of garlic toast to go with the soup.

"I'm glad I'm not having to worry about calories right now," Rachel said.

"You have to worry about getting enough of them," J.D. remarked.

Madge changed the subject. "How's the calving going?"

"Things have slacked off. It's almost as if the cows are waiting for bad weather because they know it will cause us more problems."

"I doubt that's true, J.D. After all, it's not a picnic for them, either," Madge assured him with a chuckle.

"Have you watched the weather reports today? I feel something in the air."

"I heard it this morning. There's a front coming in, but they don't think it'll be that strong. It'll lower the temps a few degrees, maybe produce some showers."

"Maybe that's what I'm sensing."

"You can tell when a change in the weather is coming?" Rachel asked, her eyes widening.

"Not always, but there are signs. Some of the old cowboys can almost call it to the hour. They have rheumatism."

"Oh."

"I think he's teasing you, dear," Madge said.

"I'd like to hear you say that when old Bluey is within earshot." J.D. laughed when Madge's cheeks reddened.

She jumped up from the table. "I think our sandwiches are ready."

Rachel watched as Madge opened the oven and took out three plates. "You cooked our lunch already on the plates?"

"Goodness, no. I just heated them up to be sure J.D. had a warm lunch before he went back outside. This is the roast beef I cooked for dinner last night. I just melted some cheese over it."

"It sounds delicious. Now I wish I hadn't eaten all my soup. I'm not sure I have enough room for this." Rachel stared at the hefty sandwich in front of her.

Madge got a butcher knife and cut Rachel's sandwich in two. "Try to eat half of it. We'll make J.D. eat the rest."

"You won't mind?" Rachel asked, looking at him for the first time.

He gave her his sideways grin. "I don't normally complain when someone gives me more food, Rachel. Especially on a day like today. That wind blows right through you."

Rachel shivered and both he and Madge jumped, immediately trying to make sure she was warm. J.D. got up and put more wood on the fire and Madge offered to put a blanket around her shoulders.

"No, I'm fine. I was just thinking about the wind J.D. was describing."

"If I told you about the blizzards we have, you'd be huddling before the fire," he told her with a smile.

"You don't really have blizzards, do you? In Texas?"

"Yeah, we do. Not too often, but the weather is much harsher here than it is in the Dallas area," J.D. assured her. Then he turned to Madge. "When is that front coming in?"

"They said sometime tonight, but they're not always on target."

"That's for sure," J.D. agreed with a snort of laughter.

Suddenly a staticky voice interrupted their meal. "J.D., we found a bunch of mamas and babies huddled in a group. We're starting them toward the barn."

J.D. leaped from the table to the counter, where he picked up a walkie-talkie. "Good job. I'll meet you halfway. Give me your location."

When he finished the communication, he turned to Madge. "I've got to go."

"I'll wrap up the rest of your sandwich," Madge said. She moved to the counter with his plate and began doing so. J.D. grabbed his sheepskin-lined jacket and shrugged into it.

"Don't you have a scarf to go around your neck?" Rachel asked.

"A scarf? What do you think I am, a sissy?" J.D. asked as he buttoned up his coat. Then he took the wrapped sandwich from Madge, kissed her cheek and slammed his hat on his head before heading outside into the cold air.

After a moment of silence, Rachel shivered again. "I can't believe it's March and this cold."

"Sometimes we have a warm March. You just never know. Have you finished eating?"

Rachel shrugged her shoulders. "I guess so. I don't have any room left. But if you'll wrap up my sandwich, I'll have it for dinner. It's delicious."

"Thanks, honey. Ready to go back to bed? I think a nap would be a good thing."

"I think you're right," Rachel agreed.

THE NEXT MORNING, Rachel woke up around nine. She knew Madge would've been up for hours, hard at work. Feeling guilty, Rachel slid from bed and went to the bathroom without disturbing the woman.

When she came back to her bedroom, she found Madge waiting, a tray in her hands.

"How did you know I was up?" Rachel asked in surprise.

"I heard you. Slip back into bed and eat your breakfast."

She did as Madge ordered, scanning the tray as it was put in her lap. "Mmm, hot chocolate. And scrambled eggs. This looks so good, Madge."

"Good. Clean your plate," Madge ordered with a smile.

"Did J.D. get off all right?"

Madge looked surprised. "Lands, yes, child. He was out of here by six-thirty."

"Oh, yes, I remember. He's an early riser."

"A rancher has to be. I'll be back in a few minutes to get your tray."

Rachel snuggled down under the covers and sipped the chocolate drink, feeling guilty that she had such warmth and comfort while J.D. was outside in the raw wind that buffeted the house.

When she finished her breakfast, she slipped out of bed again and carried her tray to the kitchen.

"Land's sake, Rachel. I would have come to get it. That's too much for you to do."

She shook her head at the housekeeper. With

graying-brown hair, Madge looked to be about sixty, but she was fit and strong and had boundless energy.

"Oh, Madge, I've done so little, and you've cared for me. And I am getting stronger. Is there anything I can do to help?"

"No, no, child, you get back in bed where you'll be warm. Maybe you should do a crossword puzzle out of that book I bought you. It will keep your brain working."

Rachel agreed and went back to her room. But she felt locked out, like a child looking through the window of a candy shop. Everyone here on the ranch was so busy, so…involved. Even when she was working, she was still uninvolved, just standing there in a certain pose, not doing something productive.

But she supposed she'd cause more trouble than she would help if she insisted now. She was still weak. Instead, she started working on the crossword puzzles, with the television playing in the background.

When the words "snow, possibly heavy" caught her attention, she looked up at the TV. Raptly she listened as the meteorologist predicted that due to temperatures much lower than originally forecast, there was the possibility of at least six inches of snow.

Rachel scrambled from her bed and went into the kitchen. "Madge, the weather report has changed. It's going to be colder and there will be snow!"

"What?" Madge asked. She immediately turned on the small television she kept in the kitchen. As soon as she confirmed the forecast, she picked up the walkie-talkie. "J.D., this is base, come in."

"Yeah, Madge, what is it?"

"The weather report has changed. Now they're say-ing temps in the twenties and six inches of snow."

"Damn! I should've known. Get the nursery ready, Madge, just in case. When is it supposed to hit?"

Madge told him it was predicted sometime in the af-ternoon, around three to four. Then she signed off.

"The nursery? What's he talking about?" Rachel asked.

"It's that small pen on the outside porch. We keep the babies in that pen sometimes, so they won't freeze to death."

"But wouldn't their mothers keep them warm?" Rachel asked. "I don't know much about cows, but—"

"The calves we keep in the pen don't have mamas. Some cows don't make it through birth."

"Oh, poor babies."

"I've got to get the bottles ready after I fix up the porch."

"Can I do something to help?"

"The bottles are in that last cabinet on the top shelf. Why don't you get them down for me?"

Rachel was pleased to have something to do, but it didn't take long. Then she went to the inner porch, a place for J.D. to clean up before coming into the kitchen. She peeked through the door to the outer porch and discovered Madge trying to tie down a canvas cover on the north end.

"Can I help you, Madge?" she called.

"Don't come out without a coat," the housekeeper warned.

Rachel hurried back to her bedroom and pulled on

jeans, a flannel shirt and a sweater. Then she grabbed her coat and stuck her feet in boots. She hurried back to the porch.

"I'm all bundled up, Madge," she announced.

"I'm struggling because the wind is so strong. We have to tie down the sides so this tarp won't blow away," Madge explained.

After tying the north end, they fastened the east side, the longer one.

"Do we leave the south side uncovered?" Rachel asked.

"Yes, so they can bring the babies in. Now I've got to spread the hay out."

There was a bale of hay on the porch, and Madge began to tear off handfuls and toss them into the small pen nearby. Rachel copied her.

When they'd finished that chore, Madge got out a heater and plugged it in not far from the pen. "That will start making the place warmer in a few minutes. Now we've got to go fix the bottles."

Rachel was delighted to be included.

Chapter Four

"Boss, you want me to take the calf up to Madge?" Bluey asked when J.D. dismounted in the barnyard.

"No, I'll take it up. Can you give my horse some oats while I'm gone? How are things here?"

"Just fine. We've got a barnful of mamas and babies." The old cowboy eyed the small red-and-white animal in J.D.'s arms. "That one's kind'a tiny, ain't it?"

"Yeah, Bluey, it is. I'm not sure it will make it. But maybe Madge can pull it through. I'll be back in a minute."

J.D. spared a hand to settle his hat more firmly on his head before he braved the cold north wind. Mixed in were tiny bullets of ice that dug into his skin. He hurried for the back porch of the house, but it was awkward to run with both his arms wrapped around the calf.

As he approached the porch he saw Madge's old hat and grinned. He'd threatened to buy her a new hat and she'd refused, saying her hat was special. He hoped having it made her calm because he'd need all her skills to pull this calf through.

"I brought you a new patient, Madge," he called as he lowered the tiny calf into the pen. The head wearing Madge's hat turned and he almost fell off the porch. "Rachel!"

"Oh, J.D., that one is so little. Did its mother die, too?"

"Uh, yeah. What are you doing out here?"

"I'm helping Madge with the babies. She showed me what to do. Hand me the new baby. I'll hold him while I feed him. He's so tiny."

"Madge!" J.D. roared. His summons brought results; Madge came running.

"What's wrong? What is it, J.D.?"

"Have you lost your mind? What's Rachel doing out in this storm?"

Rachel and Madge exchanged a look. Then Rachel said, "I'm not out in the storm. I'm on a sheltered porch with a heater two feet away from me."

"But you shouldn't be out here!" J.D. exclaimed, glaring at her for daring to be reasonable.

"J.D., I'm not that useless. I can help," Rachel said stiffly.

J.D. noticed Madge waving him away. He couldn't believe she was telling him to leave. He gave it another shot. "This has nothing to do with your usefulness, Rachel. I'm trying to do what's best for you."

"We know, J.D.," Madge said gently. "Now be on your way and find us more babies to care for."

Rachel reached for the latest arrival, already cooing to it, as if it were a real baby. J.D. stood a moment longer, watching her rub the baby calf and coax it to suck the milk bottle.

Madge awakened him from his trance. "J.D."

"Right." He walked away from the porch, returning to the wild weather outside to look for more stranded calves.

"I THINK YOU SAVED that baby's life, Rachel. I didn't think he'd learn to take the bottle."

"Do you think he'll make it, Madge?" Rachel asked, her gaze on her favorite calf.

"Yes, I do. I wouldn't have had the time to cuddle him like you did. I'm so glad you're here."

A smile broke across her face as she sat back on her heels. They'd been on the porch with the calves for hours, but Rachel felt nothing but elated. "That's such a nice thing to say. I've enjoyed it so much. For the first time in a long time, I've done something useful."

"Surely your modeling is useful."

"Not very. How desperate would you be without seeing a picture of some woman posing in clothing they want you to buy?"

Madge helped her up from the porch floor, and together they went into the kitchen. "But you make lots of money. I've read about models making millions."

Rachel gave a bitter laugh. "In my dreams. I'm not a high fashion model, Madge. I'm a print model. I'm in the catalogs, or the flyers that come with your monthly bill, trying to get you to buy more. I've made decent money, but not all that much. After my mother stole my savings, I was flat broke. But Jeff, Rebecca's husband, recovered about twenty-five thousand for me and I've been working hard ever since to put some money away. I have no retirement funds except for my savings. And models don't have long careers."

"But you're so pretty. I'm sure you can model for many more years."

"I'm not pretty now. I was under such pressure I lost too much weight and got run-down. That's why I caught pneumonia." She took off her coat and sat at the table Madge had set for lunch. When had she had the time? "You should see my twin. She's expecting a baby and she just glows."

"Was it strange, finding out you had a twin?" Madge asked as she brought Rachel a cup of her tomato soup.

Rachel took a sip before she answered. "In some ways. But I always had a feeling something was missing. I tried to ignore it, but I finally understood it when Rebecca and I were reunited. Even Vanessa, my youngest sister…we're all so much alike."

"How did they find you?" Madge asked.

"It was more like how did *I* find *them,*" Rachel said. "I was reading a local newspaper one day last fall when I saw a picture of myself. Actually, it was my twin." She went on to explain how Rebecca had been photographed at a basketball game with her son and Jeff Jacobs, a local lawyer. Once she laid eyes on the woman in the picture, all the suspicions she'd had growing up had been confirmed. Whenever she'd questioned her mother about why there'd been no pictures of her before the age of three, she'd never believed her mother's lame excuses. For Rachel, there was always a part of her that felt incomplete. After seeing the picture, she contacted the law firm, and the rest was history.

Madge had tears in her eyes. "It must be wonderful finding your family."

"Yes. It's like a promise from God that I'll never be alone again. You know, Will has found one of our brothers, too. Our oldest brother, Jim, is in the army. He's in the Middle East right now, but he's supposed to come home soon."

"I only have one sister, but we're very close. I don't have to explain things to her," the housekeeper stated.

Rachel grinned. "Exactly what I mean. They understand what I'm doing even if I'd rather they didn't."

"You're so right. Once when I was sixteen I tried to sneak out of the house to meet my boyfriend. My sister told my mother because she was worried about me. I got caught."

They both laughed at that story.

"What happened to the boyfriend?" Rachel asked.

"Oh, I married him a year later."

"You did? What happened to him?"

"He was drafted into the army and sent to Vietnam. He didn't come back. I've got his Purple Heart."

Rachel blinked back her own tears at Madge's calm recital. "Oh, Madge, I'm so sorry."

"It's all right, child," she said, taking Rachel's hand in hers. "It was a long time ago."

"And you never remarried?"

"No." Madge got up and went to the oven, checking on the cake she'd put in earlier.

Rachel watched her, sure she'd detected some color

in Madge's cheeks. Was she interested in someone? Rachel hadn't seen any sign of it. Until now.

"How many cowboys work on the ranch?"

Madge looked surprised at Rachel's question. "About ten, plus J.D. Some days they need twice that many, like today. Other days, like in winter, there's some downtime. Unless they have to start feeding the herd."

"Don't they always feed the herd?" Rachel asked, her eyes widening.

"As long as there's plenty of grass, they don't. But if it gets covered with snow, or maybe even sleet, they feed them hay. That means loading a couple of trucks with those heavy bales, then driving out in the pasture. The cows gather and they toss out the bales after they cut the wires binding them."

"I think I'd rather drive the truck than be in the back feeding the cows." Rachel shuddered at the thought. Then she grabbed Madge's old hat and slipped on her coat. "I think it's time to feed the babies again."

"You're right. But this time we can put the bottles in the holders. I think most of them will know what to do."

"Holders?"

"Didn't you see those metal things on the top rail of the pen?"

"Yes, but I didn't know what they were for."

"Come help me fill the bottles and I'll show you."

Rachel loved helping Madge, who made her feel good about whatever she was doing. When they had the bottles full and the big nipples affixed to them, they carried them out to the porch. Madge slipped one of the bottles in a metal holder. It held the bottle at an angle, pointing downward. Almost immediately the calves rushed for the bottle. Madge quickly slipped three more bottles into holders on the other side. The last one she told Rachel she could hand-feed to her favorite calf.

Rachel sat on the porch, laid a towel over her lap and picked up the baby calf. She helped it drink the milk that would give it strength and hopefully make it grow. A runt, it wasn't quite big enough to reach the bottles Madge had put in the metal holders. Besides, the other calves would push it aside.

Rachel sang a lullaby while she fed the calf. She couldn't ever remember enjoying a moment as much.

J.D. DIDN'T RETURN to the house until long after dark. As soon as Madge heard him come in, she heated up the supper she'd cooked earlier. He always had a shower on the enclosed porch and slipped on clean jeans and a shirt that he would wear again the next day.

When he stepped into the kitchen, wearing only socks on his feet, he stopped by the fire to warm up.

"Getting cold out there?" Madge asked.

"Oh, yeah. We'll have to break the ice on the stock tanks in the morning and feed the cows. We only got a couple inches of sleet and snow mixture, but I want to reward them for getting through the day."

"Good idea. Come eat your dinner."

"Have you and Rachel already eaten?"

"Yes. I sent her to bed early. She stayed up all day, so she needed the extra rest." Madge had brought to the table a hearty casserole of goulash, a mixture of pasta, cheese and ground beef that he loved. She added some hot rolls and black-eyed peas.

"You made my favorites tonight, Madge. Thank you."

"I thought after your long hours out in the storm you might enjoy them. And I have a carrot cake for dessert."

"Rachel didn't eat it all?"

Madge chuckled. "No, but she did eat a piece of it. She loved it."

The self-satisfaction in Madge's voice brought a smile to J.D.'s face. "You know everyone loves your cooking, Madge."

"I know," she replied with a grin.

"I didn't mean to yell at you today. But I was worried about Rachel being out in the cold." He stopped shoveling in his food to stare at Madge.

"She was warm enough. And I think letting her help around here will be good for her. She doesn't think she can do much that's useful."

"That's ridiculous!" J.D. said, frowning.

"That's what I said. Did you know she's been working since she was fifteen?"

"She told you that?"

"No. Vivian was filling me in last week." As she cut J.D. a piece of cake, she went on. "You know, I thought models made outrageous money. Not Rachel. She says she makes regular money. And works hard, too."

"Yeah. Apparently she's been working herself to death trying to replace her savings, which her mother stole." He went back to eating.

Madge didn't interrupt his meal again.

After the table was cleared, J.D. went through the mail that had come in that day, but he was too tired to worry about it tonight. He'd deal with it when the sun was shining.

THE MARCH WEATHER changed quickly. Two days later the sun was shining and no one who hadn't lived through it would believe the storm they'd had. The pastures were greening nicely, making feeding the cattle no longer necessary. All the baby calves were moved to the barn and given to cows with calves of their own.

"You mean the mother cow doesn't mind?" Rachel asked when Madge told her the calves were gone.

"Apparently not. It's a system that's been working for ages."

"Even Boomer?"

"Boomer?"

"I named the smallest one."

"That's not a good idea," Madge said softly.

"Why not?"

She shook her head. "Rachel, think about it. What do you think will happen to those calves?"

"I hadn't thought— You mean they'll be killed?" Rachel shrieked.

"Of course they will, honey. That's why you don't get too friendly. I learned that the hard way." Madge got down a big bowl and carried it to the table. "Today we're going to make oatmeal cookies."

"We?"

"Well, actually, you. This will be your first cooking

lesson. At least, I think it will be. You said your mother never cooked?"

"No. She was too busy managing my career." Rachel's voice was devoid of expression.

"It's never too late to learn to cook." Madge continued to move about the kitchen, gathering the necessary supplies and utensils. Then she sat down beside Rachel.

"Usually, I mix them up at the cabinet, but it will be less tiring for you if we sit down. Look at this," she began, showing Rachel the recipe she followed. For the next half hour Rachel was fascinated with the process of making cookies.

When J.D. came in unexpectedly for lunch, Madge leaped to her feet, flustered.

"J.D., I didn't know you were coming in! I'll fix you a sandwich. It won't take a minute."

"No hurry, Madge. I'll stave off starvation with some of your great cookies." He picked up one that was cooling on waxed paper on the kitchen cabinet.

Rachel's eyes widened and she watched for his reaction. So did Madge. J.D. looked up and noticed he was the center of attention. "What's wrong? What did I do?"

"Nothing, J.D. How are the cookies?" Madge asked, keeping her voice casual.

"Excellent as always, Madge." He bent over to kiss her cheek and steal two more.

Rachel let out a sigh of relief.

Madge took great pride in announcing, "*I* didn't make them."

J.D. looked at Madge and discovered she was beaming at Rachel. "Rachel made them? I didn't know you could cook," he said.

"I can't," she admitted with a shaky laugh. "Madge is teaching me."

"Well, someone did a good job," he said with a smile.

"We're going to pack a boxful and take them over to Mrs. Smith's house. Her grandchildren are visiting for spring break. They'll disappear quickly," Madge informed him.

"Hey, leave some here for me. You know oatmeal is my favorite cookie."

"We will, we will," Madge promised.

She put his sandwich in front of him.

"Aren't you and Rachel going to eat?"

"Oh, we decided to wait awhile."

Madge's offhand attitude and Rachel's blush brought J.D. to the conclusion that they'd been sampling their work. "Aha! I'm not the first one to eat cookies, am I?"

Rachel grinned at him. "Madge says it's the cook's privilege to sample what she's baked."

J.D. thought it was the first time since she'd been here that Rachel had ever teased him. She was adorable. "So that's why you're learning to cook?"

"Maybe," she replied with a wide smile.

"Are you going to eat your sandwich, young man, or just stand around gawking at us all afternoon?" Madge asked, bringing him to his senses.

"Guess I'd better eat." He sat down at the table.

"Rachel, you'd best go get changed," Madge added, sending Rachel scurrying out of the room.

"What's wrong with what she's wearing?" J.D. demanded. She'd had on jeans and a plaid shirt.

"Nothing, Mr. Fashion Consultant. Rachel said she'd like to put on a skirt for a change. I didn't see how it could hurt."

"You haven't seen her legs," J.D. muttered under his breath.

"What did you say?" Madge asked suspiciously.

"Nothing. I shouldn't talk with my mouth full," he said, and promptly bit into the sandwich.

"Uh-huh," Madge agreed. She began preparing sandwiches for her and Rachel. She didn't want to take Rachel to the neighbor without feeding her something substantial. Social calls could be tiring.

Rachel came back to the kitchen wearing a denim skirt that fitted her slim figure well, topped by a short-sleeved cotton sweater in blue that made her eyes seem larger than ever. J.D. took one look and knew he was seeing trouble. Quickly he lowered his gaze to his sandwich. He couldn't afford too many looks at Rachel. She was too tempting.

"Come eat your sandwich, Rachel," Madge called.

"I'm still not very hungry," she protested.

"I'm not having you passing out at the neighbor's house. Mrs. Smith will think I'm not feeding you properly."

Rachel sat down at once. She began eating, but suddenly paused. "J.D.?"

"Yeah?" he replied, cautiously glancing up.

"Can I go visit Boomer in the cow barn?"

In a panic, he reviewed the names of all his cowboys. With relief, he said, "We don't have a Boomer."

"She means the calf. The smallest one," Madge explained.

"You named him?" The outrage in his voice brought color to Rachel's cheeks.

"Yes, I did."

"When you live on a ranch, Rachel, you name horses, not cows. For obvious reasons."

"I haven't met any horses," she pointed out.

"You don't meet— Never mind. We've got a mare ready to foal any day now. I'll let you name her baby."

"Really? I'd love to. But I'd still like to see Boomer again." She had a stubborn look on her face.

"Okay, fine. I'll take you to the barn this evening. But you can't wear that skirt." He allowed himself one more peek at her legs. When he looked up, he realized she'd noticed.

"Uh, you might mess it up." His belated explanation didn't ring true even to his own ears. "I'd better get back in the saddle. We're having to check all the fences since we had that little storm."

After J.D. left the house, Rachel asked, "What does he mean, check the fences?"

"They ride along all the fences to make sure there are no breaks in the barbed wire. If there are, they have to dismount and repair them. Not the best job for a cowboy. Anything that means they have to get off their horses doesn't please them."

"Why?"

"Oh, honey, cowboys and their horses are a team. Besides, bowlegged cowboys don't like walking. Boots are made for riding, not walking."

"I'm learning so much, Madge. It's so exciting."

"Didn't you learn things while you modeled?"

"How to get rid of unwanted men and their ridiculous pick-up lines. And I did read a lot. There's a lot of time wasted as the photographer sets up the shoot."

"I read in the evenings. We'll have to compare notes while we drive over to Bertha Smith's house."

J.D. COULDN'T KEEP his mind off Rachel. She seemed awfully happy on the ranch. She hadn't once said she was bored, or asked to go to a mall. That would probably come when she was feeling better. She'd been proud of herself for making cookies as good as Madge's. He'd seen that and it had tickled him.

When he'd brought her out here to recuperate, he'd never thought she'd fit in so well. But she was game for pretty much anything, especially tending the calves. And she'd looked downright beautiful in Madge's old hat, the baby calf in her arms. Beautiful enough to—

"Hey, boss, don't you want to fix this break?" Doug called. They were riding fences together.

J.D. looked over in amazement. He'd missed six feet of broken fence. "Sorry," he said, swinging down from Red, his favorite mount. Doug had already dismounted with his pliers and pieces of barbed wire to connect and strengthen the break.

"Sorry, I had my mind on something."

"Yeah. I saw her in that sassy little skirt, too," Doug said with a laugh that he choked off when he met his boss's glare.

"I think you'd better forget that," J.D. said, a threat in his voice.

"Yes, sir."

Normally he wasn't formal with his men, but he didn't want any of them sniffing around Rachel. "She's our guest and will be leaving as soon as she's well."

"Right, boss. If you'll hold these two pieces of wire together, I'll twist them in place," Doug said, no doubt trying to demonstrate how much his mind was on his work.

J.D. tugged on his leather gloves to protect his hands and grasped the wires, pulling them as close together as he could. He shouldn't be too hard on Doug. After all, Doug had noticed the break in the fence. Unlike him. He would've kept on riding, his mind on Rachel.

They remounted and continued along the fence line, J.D. trying hard to keep his mind on the job. But riding fences lent itself to thinking. He had enough men that he usually sent them out in pairs, but he didn't assign any tasks he didn't do himself.

An hour later, J.D. led his partner toward home. "We've covered a lot of territory today, Doug. Good job. Along with the other two teams, we should be able to finish up tomorrow."

"Sure thing, boss."

Neither of them mentioned J.D.'s flare-up, but he felt sure the cowboy understood he was apologizing. He didn't usually praise his men for fence-riding in pleasant weather.

But then, he didn't usually daydream while he was working, either. At least, he hadn't before he met Rachel.

Chapter Five

"I'm taking you to see this calf because you're new here, Rachel, but you have to understand I'm running a business, not a petting zoo." J.D.'s voice was hard, not leaving any room for doubt.

Rachel stiffened. "So Boomer will be turned into hamburger meat?"

"That's what I'm telling you."

"So there was no point to me saving him?"

J.D. didn't answer for a few strides. Then, just as they reached the barn, he said, "I realize it may seem that way to you, but letting baby calves freeze to death isn't part of the business."

She had no response. Instead she stepped into the barn, which was filled with a fragrant mixture of hay and animal smells. She wrinkled her nose, not used to the combination.

"Should I have perfumed the cows for your visit?" J.D. asked harshly.

She turned to stare at him, her eyes wide. "What are you talking about?"

"I can tell you don't like the smell."

She shrugged. "I'm just not used to it."

"The calf you're looking for is in the fourth pen on the left."

"Are you afraid to use his name?"

He glared at her. "It's not a good idea. I told you that."

Nodding in acknowledgment, she hurried down the aisle to the designated pen. "Boomer," she called softly.

J.D. was watching to see how upset she'd be when the calf didn't recognize her. Instead, he stared in exasperation as the calf lifted his head and gazed at her, then trotted to the gate.

She stroked his little head through the boards, talking to him all the time. Then she looked around. "Can I go sit on that bale of hay and pet him?"

"If you insist," J.D. said in disgust.

About that time, he noticed the shocking prematurely white head of hair that belong to his oldest ranch hand. Bluey had come into the barn.

"Did you need something, boss?" he asked.

"No, Bluey. Rachel wanted to see the calf she handfed during the storm."

By that time, Rachel had led Boomer to the bale of hay. She was petting him and cooing to him as she had before.

"Did she tame the little feller?" Bluey asked.

"I guess so. Not that taming him changes anything."

"Did you tell her?" Bluey asked in a whisper.

"Yes."

"'Course, you could let him be your next bull."

"Are we looking at the same calf? He's a midget. I don't want to breed a herd of little cows." J.D. glared at his employee, mostly because Bluey was searching for a way to please Rachel, something J.D. had already done. But he hadn't come up with a good answer.

"I think he was born too soon. I always thought his mama was a fine cow."

"Bluey, you can't have memorized all the cows!" J.D. exclaimed.

"Not all of 'em. Just the ones I liked."

"We'll see," J.D. said as he walked toward Rachel.

Bluey followed him. "Miss, you done a fine job with this little feller."

Rachel looked up and smiled. "Thank you. He's already growing."

"Rachel, this is Bluey. He's been working here longer than I've been on earth."

"Hello, Mr. Bluey," Rachel said, holding out a hand to the man.

"No, ma'am. It's just Bluey. That's what all the fellers call me."

"All right, Bluey. I'm pleased to meet you."

"They told me you was a city girl," Bluey said, frowning.

"I am," Rachel replied, a question in her gaze.

"Well, you sure don't look like one. Them city girls are worried about gettin' dirty."

Rachel looked down at her jeans, where Boomer had slobbered. "Madge has been doing my laundry while I was sick. Now that I'm almost well, I'd better start doing it. Maybe then I won't want to play with Boomer."

"Aw, I reckon Miz Madge will go on taking care of you."

"You know her well, don't you, Bluey?" Rachel said with a laugh.

The man's weathered cheeks turned a bright red. "No, ma'am! I mean, I've heard she's a good person."

"Yes, she is." Rachel didn't say anything else because she'd already embarrassed Bluey, apparently, though she wasn't sure how.

"I've got to get you back to the house, Rachel. I promised Madge I wouldn't keep you out here for long," J.D. reminded her.

Rachel hugged Boomer and kissed his forehead. "Sorry, baby, I have to go. But I'll come see you again."

Bluey elbowed his boss. "She needs to give those kisses to someone who'll appreciate 'em, right, boss?"

J.D.'s own cheeks darkened. "Come on, Rachel. Bluey will put the calf away."

Rachel reluctantly followed J.D. to the barn door. "I don't see why we have to hurry. It's not like I'm Cinderella."

Once they were out of the building and away from Bluey's sharp eyes, J.D. slowed down. "Right. I must've been confused by your glass slippers."

She looked down at her feet, clad in an old pair of Madge's boots, with extra socks stuck in the toes so they didn't fall off. "I need to buy my own boots and quit wearing all of Madge's wardrobe."

"I have to go to the feed store in the morning to settle a bill. They have boots there. Want to go with me?"

"Oh, I'd love to. I need another pair of jeans, too. Do they have those?"

"Sure."

"I'll have to ask Madge. She may have planned another cooking lesson."

"I'm sure she can postpone it if she has. We'll ask her."

"I don't want to hurt her feelings," Rachel said urgently. "She's been wonderful to me."

"Don't you want to learn to cook?"

"Of course I do!" Rachel exclaimed. "And there's no better teacher than Madge. She makes me feel good even when I make mistakes. My mom used to— Never mind. I just don't want to upset Madge."

"She won't be upset. I promise."

"If you're sure."

They reached the porch and J.D. took hold of Rachel's elbow to help her up the steps. "I'm not ancient, J.D. I don't need your help."

He shook his head. "I was afraid you'd trip in those big boots."

"Oh. Sorry."

Madge was sitting at the table knitting something while she watched a program on her little television.

"Madge, why aren't you watching it on the big television in the family room?" J.D. asked. "I've told you before you should use it."

"I can see this one well enough. Besides, I'm fixing myself some decaf."

"Good. Can you make a cup for me?" he asked.

"Sure. How about you, Rachel?"

"I think I'll make myself a cup of hot chocolate, if you don't mind."

"Of course I don't. I'll make it for you."

"No, Madge. I won't be waited on like a guest or an invalid. I can fix my own drink."

J.D. looked at her. "Are you trying to tell me I should be pouring the coffee?"

"It wouldn't hurt you. Madge is knitting."

"Land's sake, girl. The man's put in a full day's work already."

Rachel smiled at her. "I know he has, but it's not like you've been sitting around doing nothing."

J.D. raised a hand, palm up, toward the housekeeper. "She has a point, Madge. Besides, I'm still on my feet and it looks like the coffee's ready now. You want yours black?"

"Yes, please," Madge said with a sigh.

"Oh, by the way, Rachel wants to go to the feed store with me in the morning so she can buy some boots that fit her," he added.

"That's a good idea. I was afraid she'd trip in those old things." Madge continued to knit, though she looked up briefly to smile.

"You don't mind, Madge? Did you have anything planned?" Rachel asked.

"No, I didn't, honey. We don't want to rush those cooking lessons."

"But I don't know how much longer I'll be here," Rachel said, worry in her voice.

J.D. spun around to stare at her. "What are you talking about? You're not well yet."

"Yes, I am. I need to build a little more strength, but I'm well."

Madge looked first at J.D., then Rachel. "Well, now, since I'm the only medical professional here, how about I say when you're all better? You're doing fine, but until you put on more weight and reach full strength, I don't think you can go back to the city and start work again."

"Right!" J.D. said, triumph in his voice.

"Of course not, Madge, but that shouldn't take more than a week or two."

"I would expect it to take three or four weeks, honey, but we'll play it by ear."

With a sigh, Rachel agreed. Then she began fixing her cup of hot chocolate.

J.D. gave his housekeeper a smile and a nod of gratitude.

J.D. STARTED WORK at his usual time, telling Madge to have Rachel ready about nine o'clock. He divided his men into three groups, sending each to check a different herd of steers. Steers from one herd required special feed as they were being fattened to take advantage of the recent high beef prices. Mad cow disease in Europe was suddenly making American beef preferable, which would no doubt add to J.D.'s profits.

When he returned to the house at nine, he'd already done quite a bit of work. But his mind had been elsewhere.

No matter what task he was involved in, all he could think of was Rachel. When he stocked the feed, he thought of the cookies she'd made with Madge. As he checked on the calves, his mind's eye was treated to a scene of Rachel with the runt she'd hand-fed and petted. He just couldn't seem to get her out of his system this morning. And he still had the trip to the feed store to look forward to. A time to be alone together.

What about your promise to leave her alone? a niggling inner voice asked.

J.D. well remembered his vow to Vivian when he'd taken Rachel to the ranch. He'd never intended to break it. But Rachel hadn't remained an invalid in her bed. She'd become a part of life on the ranch. His life.

He broke his stride as he walked to the house. Rachel a part of his life? With thinking like that, he'd have to tread carefully. Carefully, indeed. He didn't need to remind himself how bad he'd felt when she'd left the Stanley Ranch before.

But what could happen today? he asked himself. It was only a trip to the feed store for boots.

That flippant thought suddenly vaulted from his mind as Rachel entered the kitchen. "You can't wear that!" he bellowed.

She stared at him before looking down at her clothing. "Why not?"

Didn't she see what he saw? A tight denim skirt that hugged her curves and exposed a length of long, shapely, beautiful leg. "Because when you sit down to try on the boots, every man in a ten-mile radius will be trying to look up your skirt." His tone was harsh, due to the scene he was picturing.

Rachel blushed from her head to her toes. Then she

spun on her heel and returned to her room, slamming the door behind her.

J.D. looked at Madge. When he read disapproval in her eyes, he said, "You know I'm right, Madge. She can't wear that short skirt to try on boots."

"Whether you're right or not, I think you could've said it a little nicer." She took down a mug and poured coffee into it. "Sit down and have a hot drink. If she comes out at all, I think it may take awhile."

"What do you mean, if she comes out at all?" J.D. looked at Rachel's door, then back to Madge.

"You embarrassed her. *I* wouldn't want to go anywhere with you if you'd done that to me." Madge poured herself some coffee and sat down at the table with a sigh.

"So what do we do?" J.D. demanded as he joined her.

"We wait a few minutes. Then, if she hasn't come out, I'll go talk to her."

After ten minutes of total silence, and J.D. frowning, Madge got up and knocked on Rachel's door.

She responded at once. "I'm not going!"

"Honey, it's Madge. May I come in?"

"Yes," Rachel called through the door, her tone apologetic.

Madge slipped inside, closing the door behind her. Rachel was sitting on her bed, tears on her cheeks, still wearing the short jean skirt.

"Are you all right?"

"Yes. I'm sorry to make such a scene, but—but I didn't wear this skirt for that reason. I thought it would make it easier to get the boots on. I wouldn't have to roll up my pant leg."

"J.D. isn't too subtle; but he said that because he didn't want you to be embarrassed in public. He didn't mean to speak so harshly, you know."

"Okay, but I don't feel like going to the store with him." Rachel didn't look at Madge.

"You don't? I was going to go, too, and get some more yarn."

That snagged Rachel's attention. "You can buy yarn at the feed store?"

"We call it the feed store, but it has a variety of things for sale. There aren't a lot of choices, or the latest styles, but you can usually find something that will work for you. If not, you have to drive an hour into Abilene for any big store. Or to Lubbock, a two-hour drive."

"I can't wait to see this place. It sounds fascinating." Rachel had sat up straight, interest in her voice.

"Why don't you slip on some pants and we'll go? It's only five miles away."

"Practically next door," Rachel said with a grin.

Madge came back out of Rachel's room, pulling the door shut behind her. J.D. was still sitting at the table, nursing his cup of coffee, but jumped to his feet when she appeared.

As Madge headed for her own room, he called out, "Madge! What did she say?"

"She's coming…as long as I come, too. I'm getting my purse." She disappeared into her room.

J.D. stood there with his hands on his hips, wondering how his morning alone with Rachel, where he showed her his world, had become a threesome with Madge.

The housekeeper returned to the kitchen just as Rachel's door opened. She peeked out to be sure the older woman was there before she came forward. "I'm ready," she said, clearly speaking only to Madge.

"You look nice," J.D. managed to say, after he'd risked a quick glance at Rachel. She was dressed in gray slacks and a pink, short-sleeved sweater.

"Thanks," she muttered, but she didn't look at him. J.D. figured he'd lost all the ground he thought he'd gained since they'd parted six months ago.

"Well, let's go," he said, turning toward the door. He opened it and stood there, waiting for the two women to pass through. Then he led them to his truck. "One of you will have to ride in the back seat," he said.

Rachel immediately volunteered.

He wasn't surprised. She'd made it plain she wanted to stay as far away from him as possible. He opened the cab door, but didn't make any effort to assist her.

After helping Madge up, J.D. got behind the wheel. "Sorry for the cramped space," he said to Rachel.

"You don't have to apologize. It's not my first time in your back seat." Her voice was cool, but her words were a little friendlier.

"Yeah," he agreed, "but Betty had turned it into a bed with all those pillows."

"Yes, I slept most of the way."

"It was best, right, Madge?" J.D. asked, looking at his housekeeper.

"Yes, of course. You needed to conserve all your energy." The housekeeper sounded distracted.

"What is it, Madge?" Rachel said, leaning forward.

"What? Oh, I was thinking about what color of yarn I should buy."

"What are you making?" Rachel asked.

"A long scarf, you know, to wrap around your neck when it's cold. It's a Christmas gift."

"For one of the guys?" J.D. asked.

"Yes."

"Each year, Madge finds something nice for all the cowboys. For some of them, it's the only present they get. It makes a big difference," J.D. explained. "Let me pay for the yarn, Madge. It's the least I can do."

"All right," she agreed calmly, but Rachel stared at her, still sure something was on her mind. When J.D. looked back with a question in his eyes, Rachel shrugged her shoulders. She had to agree with him. Something was on Madge's mind, but what? Then she stared at the back of J.D.'s head. How had she understood what he was asking her? How could they have a moment of complete understanding like that when she hated him?

Hate?

A strong emotion, but at this moment it described exactly what she was feeling.

She hated him because he'd yelled at her, criticized her clothing, picked on her city ways in naming the sick calf. But mostly she hated him because he'd done his best to make sure they were never alone. From the first moment she'd arrived on the ranch, J.D. had found inventive ways to stay away. Did he dislike her so much that he couldn't stand to be with her, for fear she'd bring up their...well, their night together?

She could put his mind at rest. No way was she going to mention that mistake, she told herself emphatically.

She ignored that little voice inside her that questioned, *Was it really a mistake, Rachel, or the best night of your life?*

Instead, she stared out the window for the rest of the short drive.

When J.D. pulled into the parking space in front of the feed store, she gazed at the few buildings nearby. They included a diner, a small bank and a grocery store. "Is this a town? What's the name of it?"

"You're in downtown Prairie View."

"What fun!" she exclaimed, surprising J.D.

"You think this trip to Prairie View is fun?"

"Of course. In the city, you have to fight for a parking space and traipse around to thirty different stores to get the best bargain, or the perfect gift. Here, life is much simpler."

"Yeah, sure," J.D. said dryly as he got out of the truck.

Madge and Rachel didn't wait for him to come around and open the door for them, but met him on the sidewalk. Once they were inside the store, the housekeeper headed for the yarn display.

"This project seems very important to Madge," Rachel murmured.

"Yeah. She's not usually so intense." J.D. watched

her sorting through the colors, as if looking for a particular one.

"I think we should offer to help her. Do we have time?" Rachel asked, as if they hadn't been at odds earlier.

"We have all the time you want."

Rachel led the way across the store to the older woman's side. "Can we help you, Madge?"

She jumped a foot. "Oh! I thought you'd be looking for boots. I'm fine. I don't need any help."

Again J.D. and Rachel exchanged a glance. Rachel gulped. She couldn't believe they could understand each other so well. She must be imagining things.

"What color are you looking for, Madge?" Rachel asked, trying to put any communication with J.D. out of her mind.

"A hazel-green. You know the color—not quite green, not quite brown." She sounded distracted as she searched through a big bin of colored yarn.

"There!" Rachel said, pointing to a skein at the bottom, visible through the clear plastic side of the bin.

"Yes! That's it! Oh, I'm so glad you found it, Rachel." Madge told the salesman who approached them how much she needed.

J.D. stood there with his hands on his hips. "It sounded like she was describing the color of someone's eyes," he muttered.

Rachel wasn't sure he knew he'd spoken aloud, but she agreed with him. "Do you know anyone with eyes that color?"

"I don't really notice men's eyes," he whispered wryly.

She shrugged, avoiding looking at his brown ones. She didn't need to. She'd been seeing them in her fantasies for six months.

Whoa! She'd best not go down that road. Better to focus on the purpose of her shopping trip. Stepping closer to the salesman, she said, "Where are your boots?"

"Over against the wall. I'll be right there to help you."

Rachel guessed she'd just discovered one of the limitations of shopping in Prairie View. There seemed to be only one person to wait on the customers.

Several types of boots were displayed against the far wall. She stood there looking at them, at a loss about how to choose the right pair.

"I can help you, Rachel," J.D. said in a low growl.

She took a step away from him and replied, "I need to know what kind of boots to buy."

"If you're going to be a cowgirl, you need this type," he said, reaching past her for a black boot.

"Why?"

"The shape of the heel and the pointed toe help you keep your feet in the stirrups."

"But I don't know how to ride," Rachel said, her eyes wide.

"You will, sweetheart, you will," he assured her.

There they were, communicating with their eyes again! She had to put a stop to this. If she only knew how.

Chapter Six

When they returned home, Rachel volunteered to fix sandwiches for all three of them so Madge could work on her project.

"Oh, no, I can— Well, if you don't mind, that would be wonderful," she said. Without waiting for any response, she hurried to her room.

Rachel refused to look at J.D.

"Something seems to be going on with Madge," he finally said. "You got any ideas?"

"Not unless you have a cowboy with moss-green eyes."

"You really think she's…interested in one of my cowboys?" J.D. didn't sound as if he'd believe such a thing even if Rachel could offer proof.

Rachel looked up from the sandwiches she'd begun preparing and glared at him. "So what if she is? What's wrong with that? Why can't Madge have a little romance in her life?"

"Why are you so upset?"

"Madge told me about her husband dying in Vietnam. She's been alone for a long time. I think she deserves to find someone else to share life with." Rachel turned her back so J.D. wouldn't see the tears that had filled her eyes.

He put his hands on her shoulders and turned her around to face him. "Why does it mean so much to you?"

"I—I've been alone most of my life. My adoptive mother wasn't…warm. And I always felt something was missing. I didn't know what until I was reunited with Rebecca and Vanessa. Now, even though I'm not living in Dallas, all I have to do is pick up the phone and I can share my feelings with someone who cares about me."

To her surprise, J.D. put his arms around her. "I wouldn't begrudge Madge finding someone to share her life. She's a good woman. But I haven't seen any signs of it until today." He pulled Rachel closer so her head rested on his shoulder. "It'll be all right. I'll look at all my cowboys' eyes today and report back to you. How's that?"

She raised her head. "That will be good." Then she stepped out of his arms before she gave in to the feeling of safety…and excitement. "I'll finish the sandwiches. You have about fifteen minutes until everything is ready."

"I guess I'll work on my papers. I've got a lot of info to put into the computer."

"I didn't know you had a computer. Where is it?"

J.D. walked across the big kitchen to some shelves close to the fireplace and a big lump covered by a tablecloth. He pulled the cloth off. "Here it is. Madge believes the dust will get in it and ruin it. She covered it up before the last sandstorm we had."

"Do you mind if I use it to e-mail my sisters? That

is, if you have an Internet connection." Anticipation lit up her face.

"You know how to use a computer?"

"Oh, yes. I like to use it to organize my finances and to do research on companies I want to invest in. And, of course, to send e-mails."

"Help yourself. I've had some basic lessons, but I'm not very good at it. I'm months behind putting in the information I've collected."

"What do you use it for?"

"I track the individual cows' production, which means how many calves they have each year, the quality of their babies, etc. I keep track of which pastures I plant each year, so I can successfully rotate crops, figure how much hay I produce and how much feed I need to buy. And, of course, I keep my finances on it—if I ever get caught up putting in my bills."

"I could enter some of the information for you. It would give me something to do that wouldn't be too physically demanding…if you want me to."

"Are you serious?" J.D. asked. "It would be great for me, if you don't mind."

"I don't mind. I enjoy using a computer," Rachel said before she returned to fixing the sandwiches. While she did so, J.D. gathered up some information he wanted to have entered into the computer.

"Call Madge to lunch, J.D., please." Rachel carried various plates to the table.

"Right." He put down a pile of papers and turned toward Madge's bedroom, knocking on the door. "Madge? Lunch is ready."

When she came out, she seemed to be the same old Madge, a warm smile on her lips. "Oh, Rachel, you did a fine job fixing lunch."

"Thank you, Madge." Rachel loved the praise Madge gave her at every turn. Her mother had been highly critical.

They sat down and ate their lunch in silence. Rachel had so much to think about.

"You want to try out your new boots tomorrow morning?" J.D. suddenly asked.

She looked up in surprise. "What do you mean?"

"Your first riding lesson. If I only have a month, I should get started turning you into Annie Oakley."

Rachel stared at him.

"J.D., I don't think—" Madge was silenced by J.D. waving his hand.

"Well, Rachel?" He stood and placed his hands on his hips, as if ready to do battle. He was throwing down a challenge and expected an answer.

Rachel knew what she should say. But something in her responded to that challenge in his eyes. "Thank you, J.D. I'd like to learn to ride, though I'm not promising I'll be up to Annie Oakley's standards."

"Okay. Madge can have you afternoons and evenings, but I get the mornings, before you grow too tired. You'll have to wake up early, though. We'll start the lessons at 8:00 a.m."

Rachel swallowed. But riding would be good for her, she realized. She'd been very lazy, sleeping until nine every morning. "Okay."

J.D. looked even more surprised than she felt.

"Good. We'll start slowly, I promise." With that proclamation he spun on his heel and left the kitchen.

Rachel stared into space, still trying to comprehend what she'd agreed to.

"Are you sure about this, Rachel? Because if you're not, I can talk to J.D. He'll understand." Madge stared at her, waiting for an answer.

"I'd be crazy to turn down the opportunity to learn how to ride from a real cowboy. All my friends will be jealous." Rachel tried to smile, but was afraid her lips were trembling. "You—you don't think it's a good idea?"

"If it's what you want to do, I guess it'll be fine. J.D. will be a good teacher."

"I'm sure he will be."

J.D. was good at everything he did, she thought. *Everything.* She thought back to their night together. Yes, nobody had done to her what J.D. had—made her feel so special, so loved.

The silence was broken by Madge. "It's just that Vivian told me you were upset at seeing him again. I thought maybe you wouldn't want to be around him."

Rachel couldn't meet the older woman's gaze. She knew her cheeks were red. "We—we had a problem in communication, Madge, but I'm okay with being here. And I'll enjoy those lessons."

"It's your decision."

"May I have breakfast at seven-thirty tomorrow morning? I'll be glad to fix it."

"Don't be silly, child. Of course I'll fix your breakfast. Do you need me to wake you up, too?"

"There's an alarm clock beside my bed." Rachel managed to look at Madge and smile gamely. "I guess I'll try out my boots in the morning." She stuck her feet out in front of her. "They look good, don't they?"

Madge chuckled. "Honey child, you'll give Annie Oakley a run for her money even if you can't ride or shoot anything. You'll look much better than she did."

"Well, at least I can win one way." When the thought struck her, she felt her cheeks blanch. "J.D. won't expect me to learn to shoot, will he?"

"I don't think that's in his plans. If you were going to live here for a long time, you'd need to learn, but not for a short visit."

"Why would I need to learn to shoot?" Rachel asked with a frown.

"We're a long way from nowhere. What if someone broke in? Even if you managed to call the police, it might be half an hour before they could get here. Or what if you were out riding and a pack of coyotes came after you and your horse? Or you ran across a big rattler?"

Rachel shuddered. "But surely those things don't happen very often!"

"No, but when they do, it's too late to learn. You'll notice all our men carry rifles on their saddles."

"Oh."

"Don't worry, child, they seldom have to use them." While she talked, Madge was taking out her knitting. "If you don't mind clearing the table, I'll do the dishes later."

"I'll do them, Madge. You've done enough work for

me lately." She began stacking dishes, taking them to the sink and running dishwater.

"You can put them in the dishwasher, dear," Madge pointed out.

"I know, but there are so few, I'll just wash them. Besides, there's something satisfying about doing dishes."

The two women exchanged a smile.

After she'd finished, Rachel told Madge she was going to lie down for a little while. She had no intention of going to sleep, but when she finally stirred, the clock read four-fifteen.

She hurried to the kitchen. "Madge, I'm so sorry. I fell asleep. Can I help you with dinner?"

"Oh, no, dear. I have another casserole in the oven."

"I've got to learn those casserole recipes. They always taste good."

"Thank you, dear." Madge smiled at her. "It's just a matter of following a recipe, and you can already do that."

"Maybe. Well, if you don't need me to help, I think I'll send some e-mails to my sisters. J.D. said I could use the computer."

"I'm sure he did. He certainly doesn't want to do so."

"He said he didn't mind if I input this information on his livestock," Rachel said, pointing to a pile of papers.

Madge laughed. "He'll love you forever if you do all that work for him. It will far outweigh the riding lessons you'll be getting."

"Oh, thank you, Madge. I was feeling bad about the

free riding lessons, but I'll do his computer work in exchange. What a good idea."

Rachel sat down at the computer and soon became engrossed, first communicating with her sisters, then sorting through J.D.'s papers. She read through his files and began to find a pattern, moving quickly.

When he came in for dinner, she had several questions for him.

"Rachel, I didn't mean you should begin at once," he protested.

"Oh, no, Madge gave me the idea that I could do your computer work in return for riding lessons. Is that okay with you?"

She looked so pleased with the idea, J.D. couldn't argue. It wasn't that he didn't like the arrangement, just that she was getting the short end of the bargain. The computer work could take forever.

At least he thought so, until she showed him what she'd already done.

"Did you spend all afternoon working? I didn't intend for you to do that. You need to rest."

"I took a three-hour nap this afternoon, J.D. I don't think I'm suffering too much." She saved what she'd been working on and turned off the computer.

"I'll set the table, Madge," she said as she crossed to the table. She knew the routine.

"All right, dear." Madge was checking the casserole. "I do believe this is done," she said as she drew the dish out of the oven. "Rachel, would you put some hot pads on the table for me?"

Rachel did as she asked.

J.D. stood there, feeling out of place in his own kitchen. Rachel seemed right at home. It was a strange feeling. He'd dreamed that she would be in his house once more, but he hadn't expected to feel left out.

"Shall I fix the drinks?" he asked.

Madge stared at him, surprised. "Well, that'd be nice, J.D. Pour some milk for Rachel. We've got to make sure her bones are strong if she's going to start riding lessons."

He frowned. "Don't scare her, Madge."

She grinned at both young people. "Of course not."

"He's afraid I won't finish his computer work," Rachel teased.

"Honey, if you finish my computer work, you'll be here till Christmas," J.D. drawled. "All I'm hoping is you get me caught up a little."

"I'll do that, J.D., I promise."

The smile she gave him warmed him more than Madge's casserole.

J.D. CAME BACK to the house at eight the next morning, planning on having a cup of coffee and maybe a biscuit left over from breakfast. He figured Rachel wouldn't be ready on time. Women never were.

But when he opened the kitchen door, Rachel jumped up from the table, looking great in her new jeans and cowboy boots. Grabbing a lightweight jacket, she announced, "I'm ready."

"Uh, okay. Do you mind if I have a little coffee before we start?"

Rachel stared at him. "Okay, if that's what you want." She sat back down.

J.D. took one of the biscuits left from breakfast and looked at Rachel. "Have you ever tried jelly on one of Madge's biscuits?"

"No, I haven't," she replied.

The way her eyes rested on him, he damn near felt them to his core. What was it with this woman that they seemed to spark off each other whenever their eyes met, even in this domestic setting? "Here, I'll show you." He cut the biscuit in half, slathered it with black-berry jelly and held it out to her. "Eat."

"It's a good thing I'm not trying to diet now, J.D. Stanley, or I'd be a very unhappy woman." She followed his instructions and reached for the biscuit, but J.D. pulled it back. Then he held it to her mouth himself.

He knew this was trouble—heck, his mind kept screaming a warning at him—but he did it anyway. The second she parted her lips to accept his offering, he thought he'd drop to his knees, forget his vow to Vivian and beg Rachel to kiss him with those full, pink lips. Especially after she took a bite and then licked his finger where the jam had spilled.

"Oh my, that was really good," she said in an odd voice. Was she being suggestive? J.D. couldn't tell. Funny, how the last time she'd been at the ranch he could practically read her mind, but now he was unable to decipher her glances and tone. "Madge, you're a genius in the kitchen." The way she turned on her heel and focused her delight on his housekeeper told him that he'd totally misread her. She was talking about food, not him.

Damn, but this woman had him all out of sorts.

When Madge approached, J.D. pulled himself out of his funk.

"I'm glad you enjoyed it," she said, smiling as she wiped her wet hands on her apron. "Now, get on your way, you two. And be careful. I don't want any accidents."

"We'll be fine, Madge," J.D. reassured her. "I'm starting her out on Mandy."

"Oh, good."

"Who's Mandy?" Rachel asked, frowning.

"She's a horse. Actually, she was my first real horse. I got her when I was twelve. She's twenty years old now and doesn't run anywhere if she can walk. So she'll be safe for you to learn the basics on." He turned to Madge. "I'll have her back in about an hour."

Rachel followed him out of the house. "I only get to ride an hour?"

J.D. grinned. "By that time your body will be screaming for a hot bath."

"I may have never ridden a horse before, J.D., but I am in good shape. At least I was."

"Horseback riding uses different muscles, Rachel. We'll see how you're doing after an hour."

She found herself gritting her teeth, determined to show him how capable she was, even if she ached in every muscle she had.

She followed him to a corral where only one horse waited. "Where's your horse?"

J.D. looked at her. "My horse?"

"Well, yes, if we're going to ride, you'll need a horse, won't you?"

J.D. laughed. "Honey, the only place you'll be riding for several days will be in this corral."

"You mean I'm just going to ride around in circles for an hour? That doesn't sound like much fun to me."

"I don't remember saying it was going to be fun. I said I would teach you to ride."

She glared at him and waited silently for directions.

He climbed the fence and dropped down into the corral. "Are you going to stay out there, or are you going to join me and Mandy?"

Without a word, Rachel followed him.

"Mandy? Come here, girl." J.D. had half an apple in his hand, holding it out to the horse, who ambled over to take it into her mouth. He petted her, slapping her shoulder affectionately.

Rachel coughed when a cloud of dust rose from the animal's hide.

"Mandy likes to roll in the mud. Here, give her this when she finishes chewing." He held out another piece of apple.

"But she might bite me," Rachel protested.

"She won't if you leave it lying in your palm with your hand straight. Let her take it when she's ready."

Rachel swallowed a lump in her throat and decided to trust J.D. She didn't want him to know she was frightened.

But he obviously knew. "Relax. A horse can sense if you're scared."

"Then I'm in trouble," she muttered as the animal moved toward her. She held her hand out as J.D. had told her. Much to her surprise, Mandy's soft lips snuffled up the apple, barely touching Rachel's hand. She stared at the horse in amazement.

"Rub her nose," J.D. ordered.

"Won't she object?"

"Nope. Talk to her like you talked to that danged calf and you'll have a friend for life."

So Rachel rubbed the horse's velvety nose and cooed to her, and suddenly, she wasn't frightened anymore.

Until Mandy tried to find more apple.

Rachel shrieked and jumped back.

J.D. stepped forward and pushed the mare's head away. "Stop that, you rascal."

"What was she doing?" Rachel asked, keeping a wary eye on the animal.

"I used to hide pieces of apple in my coat pocket and she'd take 'em out. It was a game we played. She was looking for more."

"Oh."

J.D. pulled a piece of equipment from the corral fence. "Now, this is a bridle, Rachel. Here's the bit and we're going to put it between Mandy's teeth."

"We?" Rachel didn't sound enthusiastic.

"I'll do it today, but you have to watch, because soon I'll expect you to saddle and bridle your own horse."

Rachel watched as he went through the steps of doing so. When he had her pick up the saddle to feel its weight, she almost fell to the ground. "How am I supposed to put it on Mandy's back if I can't even lift it?"

"We may have to work out with weights," he said casually, and Rachel stared at him as if he were crazy.

He grinned at her. "I can help you most times, but you have to know how in case you ever have to do it by yourself."

"Okay."

"Now, see how the reins are dragging on the ground? All the horses on this ranch are trained to stop when the reins hit the ground. They'll wait for a long time. So if you get thrown from the saddle, your horse will wait for you."

"That's good, I guess."

"Sure is. You don't want to have to walk back to the barn in pouring rain in cowboy boots."

"Have you had to do that?"

"Once."

"But I thought you said all the horses—"

"That's when I made that rule, sweetheart. I didn't want it to happen to me again."

She giggled. "Did all the cowboys tease you about it?"

"Yes, they did."

"We laughed for months about that," Bluey announced from the other side of the fence, surprising both of them.

"Need any help, boss?" the old cowboy asked.

"No, I think we're about ready for Rachel to get on Mandy and ride around the corral."

"We are?" Rachel asked, her voice rising in surprise. "But I don't know how to drive— I mean, ride a horse. How do I get her to stop?"

"I'll show you once I get you in the saddle."

"What if Mandy doesn't wait for you to show me?"

"I promise she will. Trust me, honey."

Rachel looked at Bluey. "Should I trust him?"

"I reckon," the older man said with a charming grin.

Suddenly a thought struck her. Could it be...?

"Bluey, how did you get your name? It's not your real name, is it?"

"No, ma'am. My real name is Scott Williams. But when I was a young guy, I favored the color blue. All my shirts were blue, my saddle blanket was blue, my coat was blue. Whatever I needed, if it came in blue, that's what I bought."

"You must've been easy to pick out at a distance," Rachel said with a smile.

"I guess so."

"Was it to match your eyes? Are they blue?" She took several steps closer to see his eyes clearly in the sunshine.

"No, ma'am, my eyes are part brown, part green. They change depending on what color I wear."

"Oh, yes, they're very pretty."

The man's cheeks turned red. "Thank you, ma'am."

"Call me Rachel, Bluey. There's no need to be formal."

"As soon as you finish socializing, we can continue with the lesson," J.D. announced.

Rachel smiled at Bluey and moved back to J.D.'s side. "He's the one," she whispered.

"One what?" J.D. asked impatiently.

Rachel looked over her shoulder to make sure Bluey

was heading back to the barn, but still she whispered, "The cowboy with hazel eyes, the one Madge was buying the yarn for."

"You're kidding!"

"I'm not. I think he's the one."

"Well, I guess they're the right age for each other, but…"

"But what?"

"Nothing, I guess. It's time for you to get on Mandy's back."

Chapter Seven

J.D. intended to escort Rachel back to the house after her lesson, but one of his men called him away with a problem. He asked if Rachel could manage on her own.

"Oh, yes, of course," she said, holding tightly to the corral fence. "I'll be fine."

She lied through her teeth.

When J.D. headed toward the barn, she drew a deep breath. How was she going to manage to get to the house on her wobbly legs? She couldn't believe how she was trembling.

"You okay, Rachel?" Bluey asked from outside the corral.

"No, but don't tell J.D. I don't want him to know that I can hardly walk."

"Want me to help you to the house?"

"Oh, Bluey, would you? I'd appreciate it so much. Maybe I could get Madge to offer you a cup of coffee to say thank you." It struck Rachel that if she could see Madge and Bluey together, she might confirm her thoughts about them.

"I don't know about that, but I'll be glad to help you. Can you get over the fence?"

"I'll try," she said, drawing a deep breath. She managed to climb the fence, using her arms as much as her legs, and practically fell to the ground on the other side.

Bluey pulled her to her feet. "You all right?"

"Yes," she said shakily.

"Now, I'm going to put my arm around you to support you, Rachel. Lean on me."

They made slow progress toward the house. When they drew close, the back door flew open and Madge came rushing out.

"Rachel, are you all right?" she asked worriedly.

"Yes, Madge. I'm just really sore. Since J.D. had to go handle an emergency, I don't have to hide how sore I am. Bluey offered to help me."

"That was good of him," Madge said, a little self-consciously, in Rachel's opinion.

"I told him you'd offer him a cup of coffee for his efforts," Rachel added, watching both of them.

"Well, of course. And a piece of cake, too. I just finished icing it."

"Aw, I wouldn't want you to cut it just for me," Bluey said.

"I think I could use a piece of cake, too," Rachel hurriedly said, determined to provide a romantic moment for Madge.

"Good. Come on in." The woman hurried ahead of them, holding open the door.

"I'm not sure J.D. will approve of me taking a coffee break," Bluey muttered.

"If he gives you any trouble, let me know and I'll take care of it," Rachel promised. She collapsed in a chair when they reached the table.

Madge poured her a glass of milk and Bluey a cup of coffee. Then she cut two generous slices of chocolate cake.

"Oh, Madge, this is so good," Rachel said after her first bite. "Can I learn how to make a cake like this?"

"Sure you can, child. I'll teach you."

"It sure is good, Madge, I mean, Miz—"

"Madge is fine, Bluey. I don't think we should be formal."

"No, a'course not."

"So how did the riding lesson go?" Madge asked after a moment.

"She did good," Bluey said immediately.

"I survived…barely," Rachel said. "I rode around and around that corral until I thought I'd scream. My legs were screaming."

"It'll be better next time," Bluey offered.

"I'm not sure I'll be ready in the morning to do it all over again." Rachel shuddered at the thought.

"Best to get back on again right away," the cowboy said.

"He's right," Madge agreed. "But you can take a hot bath and rub liniment on your muscles. That'll help."

"Okay, Madge, if you say so. I think this chocolate cake helps as much as anything."

Bluey finished his cake and stood up to go, thanking Madge.

Rachel gave him her brightest smile. "Bluey, thank

you for coming to help me. I'm not sure I would've made it without your help."

"No problem, Rachel. If you need help tomorrow, I'll be around."

Madge followed him to the door and the two paused a moment to exchange a few words Rachel couldn't hear.

When Madge came back to the table, Rachel said, "Bluey sure is nice."

"Yes, he is."

Rachel wasn't satisfied with her response. "He seems to be in pretty good shape for a man his age."

"He's not that old. We're almost the same age. I'm sixty and he's sixty-two."

"How do you know old how Bluey is?"

Madge's cheeks reddened but she replied, "We've talked before on various occasions."

"He seems smart," Rachel added.

"Yes. I'll get the liniment while you run your hot bathwater. The hotter the better," she added as she left the kitchen.

Rachel carried her dishes to the sink and rinsed them off before loading them into the dishwasher. Then she slowly walked to the bathroom next to her bedroom. It had a generous-sized tub and she was looking forward to getting in it.

She had the tub half full when Madge arrived and poured some of the liniment into the water.

"Ooh, that smells!" Rachel protested.

"Yeah. It will really smell when I rub it on your legs after your bath, but it will help a lot," she assured her.

"Well, I guess I can stand it if it means I don't walk like someone a hundred years old. Then I can shower it off before dinner."

"You really don't want J.D. to know, do you?" Madge asked with a smile.

"Right. I really don't." Rachel would have a hard enough time facing him at dinner tonight and showing no effects of the riding lesson.

Not to mention side effects of the biscuit incident.

Even the thought of eating the biscuit from his hand made her flush. And licking his finger? Where had that come from? She'd never done anything so brazen in her life. But she had gotten caught up in the moment, caught up in trying to prove to J.D. that she could give as good as she got. He didn't think she could learn to ride or be on time, take care of herself and eat right, and she was determined to show him up.

But she'd gone too far this morning.

She got into the tub, lay back and let her worries float away.

When she climbed out later, she was surprised to find her muscles didn't ache quite so much. After Madge rubbed the back of her legs with the liniment, Rachel put on a robe and went to the kitchen to work on the computer.

As usual, she grew engrossed in her work, running through the stack of papers J.D. had left her.

"Rachel? If you're going to take a shower before dinner, you'd better hurry," Madge warned her a few hours later.

"Oh, my!" she exclaimed. She'd lost track of time.

She hurriedly clicked off the computer and rushed to her room to gather clean clothes for after her shower.

It wasn't until she was standing under the hot spray of water that she realized she'd scarcely noticed any sore muscles on her trip to the bathroom. She breathed a deep sigh of relief.

She'd just come back into the kitchen and was setting the table for supper when J.D. came in. He immediately looked at her. "Are you doing all right?"

Rachel gave him a surprised glance. "Why, yes, J.D., of course I am. Why wouldn't I be?" She thought she'd carried her response off very well, but J.D. didn't believe her.

"I suppose Madge rubbed you down with liniment," he said with a grin. "Don't worry. It will get easier." When she didn't respond, he said, "You are going to keep learning to ride, aren't you?"

She considered saying no, just because the process had involved a lot of touching, something she needed to avoid with J.D. But she refused to give him the satisfaction of thinking she wasn't tough enough to learn.

"Oh, I'm going to continue, but I'd like to know how long before I can ride outside the corral. I like a change of scenery."

J.D. stared at her for a moment. Then he said, "Well, I think one more day on Mandy. Then I'll bring in a faster horse for you to get used to."

"A new horse? I can't ride Mandy?"

"We wouldn't get much change in scenery if you stay on her. She doesn't go much faster than a walk. Don't worry. I'll get you a horse that minds her manners."

"If you say so," Rachel said, shrugging her shoulders as if unconcerned. In reality, her heart was racing at the thought of abandoning gentle Mandy for a faster horse. "I did a lot of work on the computer today. Be sure to gather what else you need inputted."

"Damn! You're fast, Rachel."

She smiled but said nothing. "Shall I fix our drinks, Madge?"

"That would be nice, dear."

When they were all seated and enjoying their meal, Rachel said, "Did you know Madge and Bluey are very close in age? He's just two years older than her."

"I didn't realize that," J.D. said, glancing at Madge before he looked back at Rachel.

Madge kept her head down, concentrating on her food.

"Bluey's a good man. He's forgotten more than I'll ever know," J.D. said.

"More potatoes, J.D.? They're your favorite, aren't they?" the housekeeper asked.

"Yes, thank you, Madge. What's for dessert tonight? I don't want to get too full if it's something good."

"Oh, it's this unbelievable chocolate cake," Rachel said.

"How do you know it's that good?" J.D. asked suspiciously.

"Bluey and I had some after my— Uh, I mean, I had a piece earlier today."

"You and Bluey had a piece?" J.D. frowned at her.

"Well, he—he helped me to the house after my riding lesson." Rachel stared at him, challenging him to say something about her weakness.

"You said you were fine!" J.D. exclaimed. "If I'd known you needed help, I wouldn't have left you."

Rachel's chin jutted out. "I didn't want you to know. I figured you'd make fun of me."

"I wouldn't have." J.D. relented when Rachel stared at him. "Well, not much," he added with a grin.

"That's what I thought," she retorted, her tone telling him how much she hated that possibility.

"It happens to everyone, honey. Your legs feel like rubber and you can hardly walk. But you hid it well."

"Madge and Bluey said it would get easier. Is that the truth?" she asked.

"Definitely," J.D. assured her.

Rachel released a big sigh. "Well, at least I don't have to pretend any longer. I'm not very good at that."

"That's good to hear," J.D. said with a grin.

The phone rang and Madge got up to answer it. Then she called Rachel to the phone.

"Hello?" Rachel said.

"Hi, Rach, it's Rebecca."

"Rebecca! I just e-mailed you today."

"I know. That's why I called. It made me want to hear your voice. Are you really doing better?"

"Yes. I had my first riding lesson today."

"But, Rach, if you're that well, why aren't you coming home?" Rebecca asked.

"Madge said I need to gain weight before I'll be strong enough to leave."

"But Betty can help you with that."

"I don't know, Becca. I'm learning a lot and—"

"But, Rachel, we miss you."

"You're doing all right, aren't you? Do you still have morning sickness?"

"No, I'm doing fine now. Vivian's feeling good, too. Vanessa sends her love. But we all miss you."

"I miss you, too, but... I'll see," Rachel finally promised. They said their goodbyes and she went back to the table.

"That was Rebecca. She wants me to come home." Rachel watched Madge's and J.D.'s reactions.

"But Madge said you needed to gain weight before you could go back to work," J.D. reminded her with a frown.

"I could go back to Dallas and not go to work." As she said the words, she considered the suggestion.

"I think you'd be too tempted to return to work," J.D. said abruptly.

Rachel didn't respond.

Madge said, "It's up to you, Rachel. We certainly wouldn't keep you here against your wishes."

J.D. glowered at his housekeeper.

Rachel relented. "Maybe I'll give it another couple of weeks, then go back. After all, I want to be there for Vivian's delivery."

"Why?" J.D. barked.

"Because I love her. She's a wonderful person and this will be an important time for her and Will."

J.D. got up from the table and walked out of the house.

"J.D., wait. You didn't have dessert," Rachel called, confused by his behavior. "Madge? What did I say wrong?"

But this time the housekeeper didn't have all the answers. "I reckon you'll have to ask J.D. that question."

WHEN J.D. RETURNED to the house several hours later, Madge was still in the kitchen, knitting.

"Welcome back," she said.

"Yeah."

"Ready for some chocolate cake? It might sweeten you up."

"I'll take some cake, but I don't think it will help my mood. Where's Rachel?"

"She went to her bedroom after supper. Said she was going to have an early night." Madge kept knitting.

J.D. went to the cake tin on the cabinet and lifted off the cover. "Do you want a piece of cake, too?"

"Yes. Will you cut me one?"

J.D. hung his head. "You were waiting for me to come in before you had your cake, weren't you, Madge?"

"I like eating with others. Makes it more festive," she agreed.

"I'm sorry. I lost my cool and thought I'd best clear out before I said something I shouldn't."

"I know, dear. But we can't control other people's lives."

"Yes, I know." He carried two plates to the table. "This cake looks really good," he said as he turned to pour two mugs of freshly brewed coffee.

"Rachel liked it this morning," Madge explained, "but she wouldn't eat any tonight."

"Think she'd want to join us now?"

"No, I think she's asleep, J.D."

"Oh. Do you think she'll come out for another lesson in the morning?"

"I assume so. She didn't say she was going to sleep late in the morning."

J.D. concentrated on his cake after that question. He did remember to praise Madge's baking, but that was the extent of his conversation.

Just before he retired for the night, Madge said, "Bluey didn't get into trouble coming in for a piece of cake this morning, did he?"

"No, of course not, Madge. I thanked him for helping Rachel."

"Thank you, J.D. Good night."

"Good night." J.D. stood there finishing his coffee as Madge retired for the night. He rinsed out his mug and put it in the dishwasher. Then he stood at the sink, staring out into the darkness.

He'd lost Rachel once. Was he going to lose her again? Maybe he should hold back, not press her now. He didn't know what to do. He was having trouble thinking clearly.

With a sigh, he pushed himself away from the counter and headed for his bedroom and a restless night.

RACHEL WOKE UP EARLY the next morning. Her muscles ached once again, but she slid out of bed and immediately began stretching. At the same time, her mind was working over the events of the day before and her sister's phone call.

Why hadn't she realized she could return to Dallas and gain the weight she needed there, with her sisters? She was no longer sick and therefore had no reason to stay away from the mothers-to-be. Had Madge lied to her? Why?

She hated even thinking such a thing about Madge. The woman had been so kind to her, praising everything she did. No, Rachel couldn't think that of Madge. Maybe she was afraid Rachel would go back to work too soon if she was in Dallas.

And that could be true.

Here, so far from the rush of life in the city, it was easy to think she had plenty of time. In Dallas, she would be reminded of the passing weeks, her lack of preparation for the future.

What should she do?

Finally, Rachel was stretched out enough to pull on her jeans and boots, along with a plaid shirt. She braided her hair down her back and put cream on her face. Then she went to the kitchen for breakfast.

"Good morning, Madge," she said with a smile.

"Morning, Rachel. How do you feel this morning?"

"Pretty good, thanks to you."

"Good. Have a seat. Your breakfast is ready."

Rachel slid into a chair and Madge put a plateful of bacon, scrambled eggs and buttered toast before her.

"I can't eat this much breakfast, Madge. You must've thought I was J.D.," she said with a laugh.

"No, honey, but I didn't want you to have any doubt about my wanting you to be fully recovered." Madge looked at her and Rachel nodded.

"I did think that for a minute or two until I realized that if I went back to Dallas, I might give in to the pressure to go back to work before I should." With a sigh, Rachel added, "I'm sorry."

"It's all right. But I truly was thinking about what was best for you."

"I know." After she'd eaten all she could, Rachel pushed away the plate, still half-full. "I can't eat anymore. Do you think J.D. will come in looking for more food?"

"Probably. That boy is a bottomless pit."

There was a knock on the back door. With a frown, Madge crossed to the door. Then she opened it. "Billy? Is something wrong?"

"No, Miz Madge. J.D. sent me to give Miz Rachel her lesson."

Madge led Billy into the kitchen. "Rachel, this is Billy. J.D. sent him to give you your lesson this morning."

"How—how nice of you, Billy. Did J.D. have an emergency?"

"No, ma'am, I don't think so. Are you ready?"

"Yes, of course." After glancing at Madge and receiving a look of concern in return, Rachel preceded Billy out the door.

The next hour dragged by for her. The lesson lacked the excitement she'd felt when she'd been under J.D.'s eye. She missed him. Why had he sent Billy in his place? She still held hope that something important had come up, that he would be her tutor tomorrow.

When the session was over, she gave Billy a stiff

smile and turned to go back to the house. But he didn't accept the dismissal. "J.D. instructed me to see you back to the house no matter what you said. He said you'd pretend not to be sore."

"I see. That's very nice of you, Billy."

She refused his assistance, but he strode along beside her, watching her carefully. Which meant that Rachel couldn't relax and limp to the house.

As soon as Billy left her at the door, she headed for the nearest chair. "Just kill me now, Madge, and put me out of my misery."

"Worse than yesterday?" she asked, sympathy in her voice.

"Yes, much worse. Billy is nice, but…he has no sense of humor. He doesn't tease me into believing I can do what I'm supposed to do. So I was tense with fear, which made the soreness that much worse."

"Why don't you go take a hot bath? I'll bring in the liniment."

"Wait. Yesterday you gave me chocolate cake. I think that helped." She gave Madge her best smile.

Madge smiled back. "Coming right up," she said as she took down the cake tin and cut a generous piece for Rachel. Then she poured a glass of milk and took it to her.

After she sat down at the table, Rachel paused and asked, "You haven't heard from J.D.?"

Madge shook her head. "No, I haven't."

Rachel finished off her cake without any more conversation. When she got up from the table, she muttered, "I'll go run my bath."

Madge called, "I'll be right in."

The rest of the day, both women waited for J.D. to make an appearance. But he didn't come in to lunch. In fact, he didn't show up for dinner on time. When he finally came in around eight, both Madge and Rachel were sure something had gone wrong.

"Are you all right?" Madge asked anxiously.

J.D. didn't look at her. "I'm fine, Madge. Sorry I'm late."

"What happened?" Rachel asked.

He glanced at her, then looked away. "What are you talking about?"

"We assumed something happened that kept you from giving me my lesson."

"Didn't Billy tell you nothing had happened?" he asked harshly.

"Yes, but—" Rachel stopped abruptly. "What did I do to make you act this way, J.D.?"

"I don't know what you're talking about." He sat down at the table. "Got any dinner left over for me, Madge?"

Rachel stood there, staring at his back. Then she said, "I'm going to bed, Madge. Good night."

After her bedroom door had closed, Madge sat down with J.D. as he ate the plateful of dinner she put in front of him. "Why?"

"Why what?"

"Don't you pull that innocent act on me, J.D. Stanley. Why did you duck out of Rachel's lesson? After all, it was your idea."

"I 'ducked out' as you put it, because I don't intend to let that woman break my heart twice."

Chapter Eight

The next week followed the same pattern. J.D. avoided Rachel at every turn. She went to bed early every night and he came in for dinner after she'd disappeared. He never showed up for her riding lesson, but made sure Billy was there every morning.

The cooking lessons also continued. Rachel was discovering a natural talent in the kitchen and on horseback, much to her pleasure.

"You know, Rachel, I've never seen anyone take to cooking like you have. I don't have a lot left to teach you," Madge told her toward the end of the week.

"Oh, Madge, I don't think I could manage on my own. It's because you give me so much confidence."

"Why don't we give you a test? Tonight you can cook dinner all by yourself." Madge looked at her expectantly.

Rachel nodded. "I'll be glad to try. And if I mess up too badly, you'll have time to cook something else before J.D. dares to walk in the door." She sounded bitter and she knew it, but the man was frustrating her. She didn't know what she'd done wrong.

"Child, you mustn't let J.D. upset you."

Rachel shook her head. "I think I should go back to Dallas, so J.D. can return to his normal routine."

"Just give him time to work things out. He'll come around."

Rachel didn't want to talk about J.D. "What shall I cook tonight for dinner?"

"J.D.'s favorite—goulash."

"Okay. Do we have all the ingredients, or do I need to go to Prairie View?" Rachel asked.

"Oh, it's all here. I keep the basics in stock in case we can't get to the store for a week or two."

"Why would that happen?" Rachel asked, curious.

"Sometimes we have rainstorms that flood the roads or take down a bridge. And in the winter you never know what will happen."

"I'm glad it's not winter. I don't think I could handle riding lessons in winter weather."

"I'm glad they're going well. Maybe I should tell J.D.— I think he'd like to know."

"He could ask if he cared," Rachel snapped. Then she apologized for her shrewish response.

"It's all right. I understand."

J.D. CAME IN THAT NIGHT after nine o'clock, even later than normal. He was tired. It had been a tough week.

When he sat down to eat, he was delighted to see there was goulash for dinner—a dinner he loved. "Thanks, Madge. I've had a hard day and this looks good."

"You should be thanking Rachel. She made dinner

all by herself." Madge stood there waiting for him to acknowledge what she'd said.

He took another bite and chewed deliberately. "It doesn't quite have the taste yours does."

Madge swatted him on the arm with a dish towel. "That's not true, J.D. Stanley. She used my recipe and it tastes just the same."

"Whatever you say," he muttered.

"Has Billy told you how well Rachel is doing with her riding lessons?"

"No." He didn't explain that he watched from inside the barn every morning as Rachel was put through her paces. He knew exactly how well she was doing.

"She's a natural."

"Did Rachel bake any rolls for dinner?" he asked, ignoring her praise of their guest.

"Oh, I almost forgot," Madge exclaimed, and ran for the oven. She pulled out a pan of rolls golden-brown on top. "Oh, good, they didn't burn."

"Perfect," J.D. said as he took one and buttered it.

"So you can praise the rolls because I baked them, but not the goulash because Rachel cooked it?"

With a sigh, J.D. said, "Everything's good, Madge, okay?"

"Okay. There's apple cobbler for dessert."

"Great."

"Aren't you going to ask who made it?"

"No, I'm just going to enjoy it."

There was no more conversation during his late dinner. When he finished the cobbler, scraping the bottom of his bowl, he carried his dishes to the sink.

"I'll do the dishes, J.D. I know you're tired. Go on and get ready for bed. You can deal with the mail in the morning. There wasn't anything important."

"Thanks, Madge," he said, bending down to kiss her cheek. "Good night."

Madge heaved a sigh of disappointment after J.D. left the kitchen. She'd had such high hopes when he'd first asked about bringing Rachel here. Things had been going well, until he heard Rachel express interest in returning home as soon as she could. That had convinced him she was going to leave him again.

Madge didn't know what had happened last time Rachel had been there, but she could guess.

It appeared this time would be no different.

"Did J.D. say anything about my goulash?" Rachel asked the next morning.

"He said it was good. And he scraped the bowl of his dessert."

"You're avoiding my gaze, Madge. I can tell he couldn't care less about my cooking." Rachel sighed. "I still think I should leave so he won't work such long hours to avoid me."

"No, Rachel, don't go yet. The work has to be done, anyway. He'll come around."

"You keep saying that, Madge, but he is one stubborn man. And I still don't know what I did wrong." Rachel took her breakfast dishes to the sink to rinse them and put them in the dishwasher.

Madge was folding clothes that had just come out of the dryer.

When the phone rang, Rachel was closest to it. "Hello?"

"Madge? I need you to take Ronnie to the doctor this morning. Can you do that?"

It was J.D.'s voice and Rachel knew he wouldn't want to talk to her. "Just a minute."

She repeated his message to Madge and she jumped up to take the phone. "J.D.? What's wrong with Ronnie?"

"He's vomiting and running a high fever."

"Sounds like the flu that's going around. I'll be down there in about five minutes." Madge hung up the phone and turned to Rachel.

"If it's the flu, as I suspect, probably half the bunkhouse will come down with it. I've got to take Ronnie to the doctor in Abilene. I'll be gone until lunch. Can you handle things here for me?"

"Sure," Rachel said calmly.

"Thanks so much, Rachel. It's such a relief to have you here to back me up."

She smiled. "The only reason I can is because you're a good teacher, Madge. Be careful," she added as the housekeeper pulled on a sweater over her short-sleeved shirt and grabbed her purse.

Rachel took her lesson with Billy, riding outside the corral for the first time. She loved it.

Then she hurried back to the house. First, she put a load of clothes into the washer, then she got out the recipe for carrot cake and followed it exactly.

About the time she got the cake out of the oven, the washer finished and she put her clothes in the dryer.

Then the phone rang.

"Hello?" she said again.

"Is Madge back from the doctor?"

"No, she's not. Can I help you?"

"Uh, I'm the cook at the bunkhouse and I got three guys down. They're throwing up a lot and I think they're dehydrating. And I don't feel so good myself."

"All right. I—I'll try to get hold of Madge."

Rachel disconnected immediately and dialed Madge's cell phone. She filled her in on what was happening at the bunkhouse, and Madge gave her the bad news.

"It's the flu, a severe strain. I'm going to get supplies now. I'll buy lots of Gatorade and some of those masks for us to wear. Don't go down there, Rachel. I don't want you to get sick, too."

"But, Madge—"

"Don't go down there."

"All right, I won't. How do I call the bunkhouse?"

Madge gave her the number. "I'll be there in an hour and a half, I promise."

"Okay."

Rachel hung up the phone and searched in Madge's large pantry. She thought she'd seen some Gatorade in there. She found two big containers of it, and called the bunkhouse to arrange for someone to come pick them up.

A couple of minutes later, when one of the men knocked on the back door, Rachel gave him the bottles and some paper cups. "Tell them to try to drink it. We don't want them to get dehydrated."

"Yes, ma'am."

"How many men are well?"

"Uh, I guess six of us and Cook."

"Hmm, I don't think you should count on Cook. We'll figure out something for dinner."

"Yes, ma'am," he said, and went off with the Gatorade.

By the time Madge got home, Rachel had worked out some plans. "Madge, we should keep the men separated. If we have six well ones, do we have a place they can stay?"

"We have three extra bedrooms here. They could double up. With the cook down, we'll need to fix supper for everyone. I'll make a big pot of vegetable soup for the sick ones. They might be able to eat that."

"And I can triple the recipe for goulash and make it again tonight for the rest."

"Can you handle dinner here, if I go to the bunkhouse?" Madge asked worriedly.

"Yes, of course. Someone will have to tell J.D. and the others so they won't go into the sickroom."

"You're right." Madge crossed the room to the walkie-talkie and picked it up. "J.D., this is base. Come in, please."

"Yeah, Madge. What is it?"

"The flu. We've got three men sick in the bunkhouse, and Cook doesn't feel well. Have the six well men come here to eat and sleep. It's the only way to avoid everyone going down."

J.D. groaned. "Okay, we'll be in by seven. It's clouding up out here and we're not going to be able to see much past that."

"We'll have dinner on the table waiting."

Madge replaced the walkie-talkie and took out a large stock pot.

"Madge?"

"Yes, Rachel?" Madge asked as she began to gather the ingredients for her vegetable soup.

"Why did you tell J.D. *we* would serve dinner here?"

"I wasn't trying to mislead him. If I'm not back from the sickroom, you'll serve it by yourself, but I expect I'll be back. Those men don't like women in their bunkhouse."

Rachel knew if she was sick, she'd want Madge taking care of her. But she wasn't going to argue. Instead, she asked where clean sheets were stored so she could start making up the beds the men would need.

Madge wanted her to wait until she could help her, as soon as she got the soup started, but gave directions for finding the sheets and the bedrooms they would use.

"If necessary, I can give up my room and share yours," Rachel offered.

"No, we have three more bedrooms. This house was built for a big family."

"It's a wonderful house," Rachel said over her shoulder as she set off to prepare the rooms.

Madge caught up with her in the third bedroom. "How are you doing?"

"Fine. The bathrooms will need more towels. I didn't know what to do about that."

"I have some stored away. I'll get them and put them in the baths."

Rachel finished making the queen-size bed and gave

a sigh. She enjoyed doing housework. Unfortunately, there was no money in that.

She went back to the kitchen. Already, the soup was giving off a delicious smell.

"What else do we need to do?" she asked Madge.

"Well, I'm going to go work in the barn for a couple of hours."

"Doing what?"

"The men who were left behind were supposed to feed the animals in both barns and clean out the stalls. I won't be able to get all of it done, but I can start."

"I'll come help. You'll get twice as much done."

"Oh, no, Rachel, that's too hard a job for you. Besides, you have to cook dinner tonight."

"Madge, it's one o'clock. Let's have a quick lunch, then we can work until five. By then you'll need to take the soup down to the bunkhouse, and I can start dinner."

"Are you sure?"

Rachel couldn't resist hugging her. "I'm sure."

After eating sandwiches, they went out to the barn. A quick learner, Rachel followed in Madge's footsteps, feeding the animals and cleaning each stall on her side of the barn. Scooping up manure and loading it into a wheelbarrow was a new skill, but she worked hard.

Madge dragged down a bale of hay and cut the wires so they could spread fresh hay, too.

They finished the first barn by three-thirty. They raced to the second. Rachel figured it wouldn't take as long this time, because she now knew what to do. They hurried through their work and finished right at five o'clock.

"Rachel, you worked like a demon! I am so proud of you."

"Thanks, Madge. Let's hurry home. I want to grab a quick shower before I start cooking."

Madge grinned. "I figured you would."

As the two women rushed back to the house, Madge kept throwing glances over her shoulders.

"What are you looking at?" Rachel asked.

"J.D. said something about it getting dark early. I think he meant those rain clouds. We may have a gully-washer tonight."

"Gully-washer?"

"A big rainstorm that fills up the gullies, making them run like creeks."

"Oh, my. That kind of rain must be a problem."

"Can be."

They each hit the showers, and ten minutes later Rachel was preparing dinner and Madge was carrying the big pot of vegetable soup to the bunkhouse. She'd given Ronnie several big containers of Gatorade when he went back to the bunkhouse to go to bed earlier.

Now she carried Tylenol in her pocket for everyone to keep their temperatures under control. She'd put the rolls in a plastic sack that dangled from one wrist as she gripped the soup pot. She'd already tied on a face mask, hoping to not catch the flu herself.

Rachel, meanwhile, made dinner and set the table for seven people—J.D. and his men. She figured she'd eat before they came in, and Madge, too, if she got back that soon.

Exactly at seven, as she put one of the casserole

dishes on the table, the back door opened and she heard J.D. ordering his men to wash up at the sink.

When he entered, she asked him at once what she should serve the men to drink.

Instead of answering her question, he asked one of his own. "Where's Madge?"

"She's still down at the bunkhouse tending to the sick men."

"She shouldn't be doing that," J.D. muttered. He circled Rachel and made a direct path to the phone.

Rachel greeted the other men and got them settled. She didn't hear any of J.D.'s conversation until she started pouring tea beside him.

"Fine!" he yelled, and slammed down the phone.

She said nothing, turning and taking the drinks, two at a time, to the table.

"Rachel," he said harshly, bringing her to a halt. "You don't need to be serving us. Go to your room."

She ignored him. She set down the glasses she was carrying with a smile and went back for the next two.

He stepped in front of her. "Didn't you hear me?"

She'd just about had it. "Yes, I did notice your rudeness, but I chose to ignore it. I hope Madge did the same, because after spending all afternoon feeding the animals and cleaning out their stalls so you wouldn't have to, I think we should be treated with a little more respect!"

Then she crossed to her bedroom and slammed the door shut behind her.

J.D. stood there, not knowing what to say. He and his men had been so glad that the barns were cleaned out that they hadn't questioned who'd done it.

"You mean her and Madge did all that work for us?" one of the cowboys asked.

Bluey nodded. He stood up. "I reckon I'll go see if Madge needs any help."

J.D.'s booming voice stopped him. "Sit down and eat, Bluey. I'll go take care of Madge. As soon as I apologize to Rachel."

He went over and knocked on her door. No matter how quietly he spoke, he figured his men would hear their conversation. "Rachel?"

No answer.

"Rachel, I need to apologize. Then I'm going down to see if I can help Madge. Please open the door."

She opened it about two inches. "Yes?"

"I was wrong to be so rude to you. Dinner looks really good and I'd guess you made it all on your own. Thank you for all you've done today."

"You're welcome."

"I'm going to the bunkhouse, if you don't mind keeping an eye on my men in case they need something."

"I'll be glad to," Rachel said quietly.

She waited for him to walk away from her door before she opened it and came out. The men hadn't served themselves, afraid they shouldn't.

As J.D. left the house, he heard her assuring them that they should go ahead and eat, that she had plenty more in the oven.

Chapter Nine

Madge looked up as he entered the bunkhouse. "J.D., what are you doing down here? Here, put this on," she quickly ordered, holding out a disposable mask.

J.D. took the mask and tied it on. "I came down to see if you needed any help. Do you?"

She put her hands on her hips and looked around the bunkhouse. "No, and there's no need for me to stay longer. I've given everyone Tylenol and Gatorade. I've served them all vegetable soup. Most of them kept it down, too. So I guess I'm ready to come eat my dinner."

"Good. I know the men appreciate your efforts, Madge."

"I'm not sure they'll even remember I was here. This type of flu sure is tough."

"Yeah," he agreed with a sigh. "Let's go have dinner before the others eat it all. By the way, thanks for your hard work this afternoon."

"Who told you?" Madge asked, surprised.

"Rachel. I—I was rude to her, and she blasted me across the room."

"Good for her. She's been wonderful, J.D. I wouldn't have been able to finish if she hadn't come with me and worked nonstop."

"I know." He held the door to the bunkhouse open for Madge even as he removed the mask from his face. "Do you think these things work?"

"I hope so. The men are so miserable. I sure don't want to go through their agony."

J.D. took her arm and escorted her the short distance to the main house. When they entered the kitchen, he noticed Rachel had already set a place for Madge. As they came in the door, she took the other dish of goulash out of the oven and put it on the table. Then she replenished the bread basket.

"Tea or coffee?" she asked.

"I'll get our drinks, Rachel," J.D. said. "You sit down and eat."

"I ate before you got here. Madge, what do you want to drink?"

"I'd love some coffee. The wind has turned chilly."

"Has the rain started?" Bluey asked. He happened to be sitting beside Madge.

"Not yet, but I don't think it'll be long." As if on cue, lightning lit up the sky, followed almost immediately by a loud roll of thunder. "Oh, my!"

Rachel gasped. "That must've been very close."

Several of the men agreed.

Billy looked up and said, "I don't think I'll be able to give you a riding lesson tomorrow, Rachel."

"That's all right, Billy. We should probably postpone any lessons until after we've gotten rid of the flu."

"Yeah," Billy agreed, but he looked at J.D. rather than Rachel.

She took down the cake tin and put it on the counter. When she removed the lid, she heard several murmurs of appreciation behind her.

She smiled at the men. "I didn't want you to eat so much you had no room for dessert. Let me know when you're ready for a piece."

Several men volunteered to go first, and Rachel took away their dirty plates and put a big slice of cake on a saucer before each.

When J.D. finished, he stood up. Rachel came to take his plate. "I can put my plate in the dishwasher, Rachel. You must be dead on your feet with all you've done today."

"I think I have enough strength left to cut you a piece of cake."

"That'll be fine as long as you cut one for yourself."

She nodded. "Okay. Madge, are you ready for dessert?"

"I'll take just a small piece, Rachel, please."

"You cut the cake. I'll get her dishes," J.D. said.

After he did so, he waited for Rachel to sit before resuming his own seat.

Rachel sat down opposite Bluey, since the cowboy sitting there had finished his dinner and gone off to bed.

"This sure is good cake, Madge," Bluey said.

"Rachel made it while I took Ronnie to the doctor." She shot Rachel a smile and turned her attention back to Bluey. "You should see those poor guys in the bunkhouse. They're miserable."

"I bet they're better since you spent some time with them," he said staunchly.

"Thank you, Bluey," Madge said with a blush.

At that exchange, it was all Rachel could do not to give J.D. a telling look. She was right. something was brewing between those two.

When dinner was over, J.D. volunteered to clean up. "Madge, you and Rachel go on to bed."

Rachel spoke up. "I'll do it. Both of you should go to bed. You're the ones who have to make an early start in the morning."

The other two reluctantly agreed.

It didn't take Rachel long to finish cleaning up the kitchen. She turned out the lights and headed for her bedroom, ready to drop. But before she went to sleep, she set her alarm to get up at six to help Madge with breakfast. Morning, she knew, would come too soon.

MADGE HAD JUST PLUGGED IN the coffeepot when Rachel entered the kitchen the next morning.

"What are you doing up so early?" the housekeeper asked.

"I wanted to help you with breakfast. You've got a lot of people to feed."

"I could manage."

"Of course you could, Madge. I know that. But I'd feel like a lazy person, sleeping late while you fix breakfast for all the men and then head down to the bunkhouse. That's what you planned on doing, isn't it?"

"Well…" Madge shrugged her shoulders.

"So let me help you."

She gave her a hug. "You're such a good person, Rachel."

"Since I'm so good, do we have time for a cup of coffee before we get started?"

"I hope so. I need the caffeine."

"You're not the only one," J.D. said from the doorway. "I got up early to help you, Madge, but it appears you already have a helper."

"Yes, I do. We're going to have a cup of coffee first. Want to join us?"

"I sure do. I'll even let you serve me," J.D. said, taking a seat at the table. Rachel brought J.D. his coffee and carried her own to her seat just as Bluey came into the kitchen.

"Bluey, are you ready for breakfast already?" Madge asked in surprise.

"No. I thought I'd get up and help you."

Madge beamed. "I must be living right." She took down another cup. "Sit down and join us."

For the next ten minutes the four of them talked quietly about nothing important, but Rachel thought it was the first time in a week that J.D. had treated her like she was alive.

Then she and Madge began cooking. While Madge mixed biscuits and got them in the oven, Rachel fried bacon and sausage. The two men set the table, and when the others drifted in, they poured cups of coffee.

In no time breakfast was on the table, the men relishing the hot food. With the leftovers, Rachel made biscuit sandwiches and put them in plastic bags, handing each ranch hand a doggie bag. Since they expected more showers today, those snacks might be the only things dry on them for the rest of the day.

As soon as the men were out the door, she and Madge started on pancakes for the sick hands.

After Madge left to deliver the breakfast, Rachel got the dishwasher going, mopped the kitchen floor and started a load of J.D.'s clothes, along with a few of her things and Madge's.

When the phone rang, she picked it up to hear Madge's cheerful voice. "How are you doing, Rachel?"

"Fine." She told her what she'd done so far, and asked if there was anything she could do at the bunkhouse.

"We're fine here. You just enjoy your day."

Rachel did just that. She puttered in the kitchen, making two chocolate pies, and finished the laundry. She loved the smell of clean clothes.

About five, finding herself with some free time, she switched on Madge's little television to catch the evening news.

When the weather came on, she leaned forward intently. The radar showed more rainstorms coming their way. It looked as if the cowboys would have an uncomfortable time for several more days.

She walked over to look out the window toward the barn and, to her surprise, saw the cowboys ride in. When she noticed several of them being supported by others, she knew they either were injured or were more flu victims.

Since it would be awhile before they got to the house, she put on a big pot of coffee. Then the phone rang. It was J.D. "We've got a couple of guys sick, Rachel, so there will only be five of us and you and Madge for dinner."

"All right. Is there anything I can do?"

"No, Madge doesn't want you down here. I'm sending the rest of the men up there. They might like to take a hot shower before dinner if that's possible."

"Of course." She'd restocked their baths with towels already.

When the men reached the kitchen, leaving their wet outerwear on the back porch, she told them they had time to grab a hot shower before dinner if they wanted. There was a mad rush to the bathrooms.

When they returned to the kitchen, they were wearing the clean clothes Rachel had washed and folded that day. They all made a point of thanking her.

"I'm glad to do it. I got to stay inside all nice and dry. It only seemed fair to do that for you." She started pouring cups of coffee, something else the men appreciated.

When she opened the oven and the aroma of her pot roast filled the room, the men all rushed to the table. They were passing around the dishes when the back door opened for J.D. and Madge. He opted for a hot shower before eating, but Madge sat down with the rest of them, updating them on their co-workers' conditions.

When J.D. came to the table, cleaned up and changed, everyone passed food to him. When they were all once again eating, the cowboys made it a point to let J.D. know that Rachel had done their laundry and made this delicious meal.

Rachel was actually embarrassed by their compliments. She shook her head at J.D. as he started to add his own praise. She could feel her cheeks heating up when he gave her a long look. Throughout the rest of the meal and cleanup, she avoided his eyes.

When everything was done, he surprised Rachel by saying, "Now I'll serve you two ladies some pie."

They both protested, but he ordered them to sit. He brought them each a cup of coffee and poured one for himself. Then he cut three pieces of pie and joined them at the table.

"How are you two holding up?" he asked after a minute.

"Fine," Madge said. Rachel nodded.

"I'm asking because it looks like it's going to be a few days before we're back to full strength. And it just so happens the weather is going to be lousy about the same length of time. Do you want me to hire some help?"

Madge shook her head. "If it was just me by myself, I'd need help. But Rachel has been filling in for me here and I've been able to look after the sick ones."

"But she's supposed to be putting on weight and recovering from her illness." J.D. looked at Rachel. "Do you want to go back to Dallas now?"

"And leave Madge to do all this by herself? Of course not. I'm actually enjoying it. I guess I shouldn't admit that, but I'm trying out new skills. It amuses me when I manage to do something right."

Madge patted her arm. "Child, you're doing everything right. I don't know what I'd do without you."

"Thanks, Madge."

"I owe you a big thank-you, too, Rachel," J.D. said. "When you're ready to go back to Dallas, just let me know."

She couldn't help the disappointment she felt down deep at J.D.'s easy offer to drive her home. She'd hoped he would have wanted her to stay. The last time she'd visited his ranch they'd spent as much time as possible together. It was so different now....

Without another word J.D. took their plates and put them in the dishwasher. "Well, ladies, let's go to bed."

THE REST OF THE WEEK was a struggle. Rachel actually felt guilty because she enjoyed meeting the demands. It built a real self-confidence that she'd never felt before. She did miss getting to ride horseback, but it couldn't be helped.

By the end of the week, however, J.D. had only Bluey and Billy left standing. It would just be for a couple of days, since some of the earliest down would be back on their feet soon. But for those two days, J.D. needed help.

Madge offered to ride out with them, but J.D. refused, saying she was needed taking care of the sick.

"Well, Cook's doing better. They really don't need me down there much."

"Then why don't I ride out with J.D., and you can take over here?" Rachel suggested.

"Whoa!" J.D. roared, coming out of his chair. "I'm not taking you out to work the cows. You'd get hurt."

"Why don't we ask Billy? He's my teacher. He would know better than anyone."

Billy, who was still sitting at the table, as was Bluey, swallowed and shot a panicky look around the room, as if wondering whom he could get to bail him out.

"Well, Billy?" J.D. asked.

"Well, boss, I, uh, I have to say I think Rachel is pretty good on a horse. It's not like she'd have to do anything dangerous. We'll be moving that herd just a couple of miles away. She could ride drag. You could take point, and me and Bluey could ride up and down the sides."

"That'd work," Bluey murmured.

J.D. glared at both of them, then at Rachel. "You'll have to do exactly as you're told. Do you understand?"

With a demure smile, she said, "Yes, boss."

"Have you got a slicker?" he demanded.

"No, but—"

"I'll get her one," Bluey said, interrupting her.

"Dress warmly," J.D. commanded.

"Okay."

"Madge, can you figure out some lunch to send with us in the morning?"

"Sure thing."

J.D. left the table first that evening. The other two men followed him.

"Are you sure you can do it?" Madge asked anxiously.

"No," Rachel said with a smile, "but I want to help out. I'll be all right. Billy will help me."

"And so will J.D.," Madge said.

Yeah, she thought, and that was part of the problem.

J.D. HARDLY SPOKE to Rachel until they reached the barn the next morning.

Bluey handed her a slicker.

"Tie it down good to your saddle," J.D. ordered. "Put your lunch in your saddlebag. Most important of all, let me know when you've had enough or need a break. You won't help us by falling out of the saddle."

"Yes, boss," she said, holding back a grin. She was as excited about today as she had been about testing her cooking and housekeeping skills.

She was riding the young mare Billy had put her on when they'd ridden out of the corral. After she mounted, Billy rode up beside her.

"Rachel, these are cutting horses. If a cow breaks from the herd, it's the horse's nature to go after it. If your mount does that, grab hold of the saddle horn and don't let go, okay?"

"I won't, Billy. I won't embarrass you, I promise."

"I'm not worried," he assured her with a grin.

She waited until he guided his horse out of the barn, and she followed on Rocky. Billy assured her the mare got her name because she was as easy to ride as sitting in a rocking chair. Rachel doubted that.

J.D. came up beside her.

Rachel felt sure he was there to give her another lecture, but he simply rode along beside her. When she finally dared look at him, he gave her a nod and kept pace with her. She took that as encouragement.

Today she was a cowboy!

Chapter Ten

By noon, Rachel's enthusiasm had diminished some-what. She was still proud of being able to help in a cri-sis, but she felt numb from her waist down. She'd never been on a horse for such a long period of time.

Fortunately, her job was fairly easy. She had to stay in the saddle and bring up the rear of the herd. The other three were gathering the animals, adding to the num-bers. The thunderstorms had scattered the cows more than J.D. had expected.

Rachel reached back to her saddlebag and drew out the sandwich Madge had made for her. There was also a candy bar for instant energy, but she thought she'd better save that for later in the afternoon.

She munched her sandwich while she sat on her horse, moving slowly behind the herd. The food tasted good and she relaxed more than she should have. When a cow decided to leave the herd, Rocky took off after it. Rachel dropped her sandwich and grabbed the sad-dle horn just in time to remain in the saddle.

Fortunately, she'd managed to keep hold of the reins

in her right hand, and brought Rocky to a stop so she could gather herself. Then they continued on after the runaway cow. Rachel was proud of getting the cow back to the herd, but she regretted the loss of her sandwich. At least she'd managed to eat some of it before she dropped it.

"You okay?" Billy called.

Clearly, he'd seen her escapade. She waved back to him, smiling at her mentor. She'd promised she wouldn't embarrass him…but she almost had. She resolved to remain alert. Fortunately, J.D. was up near the front of the herd and hadn't seen her almost lose her seat.

She thought she couldn't be more miserable, but then the rain started. She pulled Rocky to a halt and untied her slicker as quickly as she could. She was already wet when she finally got it on, tucking her braid up under the hat Madge had loaned her.

By that time Rachel was ready to eat her candy bar. She pulled Rocky to a halt and got the candy out of the saddlebag, staying on alert so she wouldn't be surprised by a wayward cow.

She had a growing admiration for the job cowboys did. J.D., Bluey and Billy were still gathering errant cows, working twice as hard as she was, even in the rain. She wanted to crawl into a nice warm bed and stay there for a week or two.

Rachel pictured a hot, steaming tub, and she almost fell out of the saddle with a yearning that surprised her. The contrast to the cold rain made her lose her concentration for a moment.

When Rocky started after another cow, she grabbed

the saddle horn, saving herself again. After she brought that cow back to the herd, she had to push them forward. The animals were stringing out too much, which made more work for Bluey and Billy.

By the end of the day, around six o'clock, they got the herd into the pasture J.D. wanted them in. He signaled it was time to go home, and Rachel almost sobbed with relief.

J.D. rode up beside her. "Rachel, you did a good job today. I want to thank you."

She avoided his gaze. "You're welcome."

"Are you all right?"

"I'm tired."

"Can you make it back to the barn?"

She glared at him, then assured him she could make it to the barn. Her legs were screaming, but she wasn't about to let J.D. know that.

When they reached the barn, Rachel sat frozen on her horse, afraid to get off because she knew she'd fall flat on her face if she did.

J.D. appeared beside her. "What's wrong, Rachel?"

"I—I can't get off. I won't be able to walk," she told him, unaware that tears were rolling down her cheeks.

"Damn. I knew I was asking too much. Come on, honey, slide into my arms. I won't let you fall."

His gentle tones persuaded her as much as his strong arms. She fell off Rocky into his embrace, and he shouted for Bluey.

"Take care of Rachel's horse. I'm going to get her to the house. Then I'll come back and help."

Billy stepped forward. "We can manage, boss. We'll be up for dinner in a little while."

"Thanks, guys," J.D. said, and started toward the house, carrying Rachel.

"I'm sorry, J.D.," she whispered.

"It's all right, honey," he said, his voice husky with emotion. "You did a great job," he added, holding her even closer.

She lay her head on his shoulder, a sigh of contentment escaping her lips. She was in a miserable state, but she felt as if she'd died and gone to heaven. Being in J.D.'s arms was all she'd wanted. For days. For months.

When they reached the house, he put her down to open the back door. He intended to pick her up again, but instantly she came to her senses.

"I think I can walk now, J.D. I don't want to scare Madge."

"All right. I'll keep my arm around you just in case you can't make it."

Madge met them at the door because she'd heard them on the porch. "Rachel, are you all right?"

"Of course, Madge. I just need to have a hot bath before dinner. But I'm starving. I hope you fixed something good." Unfortunately, her voice wobbled as much as her legs, and Madge reached out for her.

"I'll get her in a hot tub, J.D. It'll revive her quickly, I promise." She escorted Rachel to the bathroom.

"I helped them, Madge, but it was hard work. It always looks so easy when they ride. They do it so well. Am I rambling?"

"Maybe just a little, honey. Come on now. You start taking off your clothes while I start the water running."

Rachel struggled to undo the slicker she'd worn to keep out the rain. Madge stood and helped her.

"It must've been hard out there."

When Rachel lowered herself into the tub, she moaned as the hot water hit her tense muscles. Then she closed her eyes and sank back against the rim. "Oh, Madge, this feels so good."

"I guess it does. I'm going to go put dinner on the table. Don't stay too long. I made green enchiladas for tonight."

Rachel's stomach growled. She had intended to stay in the tub forever, but her hunger was telling her to head for the dinner table. After soaking for about fifteen minutes, the cooling water and her desire for food had her getting out, drying off and dressing in cozy, warm clothes.

She got to the table just as the men came in. She apologized for not taking care of her horse, but they assured her it was no big deal.

As they ate, the men talked about tomorrow. Rachel suddenly realized they were trying to figure how to manage with just the three of them. "I'm going back out tomorrow," she stated.

"No, you're not," J.D. said firmly.

"Was I that big a handicap today? You said I helped."

"Of course you helped, but you couldn't even walk when it was over," he exclaimed. "I'm not letting you do that to yourself again."

"But, J.D., it will just be for one more day, and the

second day will be easier." She saw refusal in his face. "Won't it, Billy?"

"Probably. It takes awhile to get used to riding all day. But you did a good job today, Rachel."

"Thanks, Billy. See, J.D.? You'll have your regular cowboys back soon. I'm just filling in."

J.D. shook his head and asked for a piece of cake.

Rachel repeated her intentions more emphatically. "I'm going out tomorrow, just like today. I'm not an expert, but I can make it for one or two more days."

"This is good cake, Madge," J.D. said, completely ignoring her.

"Boss, how are we going to manage, just the three of us? This herd was scattered all over the place. If we didn't have Rachel pushing from behind, we wouldn't have managed. The other herd will be just as spread out."

Billy's impassioned plea didn't seem to have an effect on J.D., so Rachel was surprised when he relented at last.

"Okay, if she can get out of bed in the morning, I'll take her. But Bluey will point the herd this time. I'm hanging back on the side so I can keep an eye on her."

"Why are you going to do that?" Rachel retorted. "I made it, didn't I?"

"I'm letting you come. Don't push your luck," J.D. warned, glaring at her.

She took his advice and ate her chocolate cake and the glass of milk Madge had insisted on giving her. Even with all the activity, she figured eating like this would definitely help her put on weight.

But her weight and health weren't on her mind when she took to her bed later on. Worries about riding—and being watched by J.D.—kept her up most of the night.

When the alarm went off at six the next morning, Rachel was afraid she couldn't climb out of bed. It was a struggle, but she managed. She took a hot shower and almost forgot to get out of it and dress. She didn't reach the kitchen in time to help Madge, but at least she got there.

J.D. was sitting at the head of the table and he watched her carefully as she walked in. "You okay this morning?"

"Sure, I'm fine," she answered. It surprised her to discover that she really was. Half an hour earlier, she would've sworn she'd never feel good again.

With a smile for Madge, she ate her breakfast. "Working outside certainly does improve your appetite, doesn't it?" she said, looking at Bluey and Billy. They were both quiet this morning. "You two aren't getting sick, are you?"

"Not me," Bluey said at once.

"I hope not," Billy said with a lot less conviction.

Madge jumped up from the table and walked around it to feel Billy's forehead. "You're running a fever."

"Not much. I'll take something for it. I can't leave J.D. even more shorthanded today. Tomorrow a couple of the guys are going to be able to ride out again."

"Are you sure you can make it, Billy?" J.D. asked, frowning.

"I'm sure."

Rachel hurriedly finished her breakfast, then grabbed

her slicker and Madge's hat, adding a sweater over her T-shirt. "I'm ready," she announced. J.D. was the only one waiting for her.

"Come on. The guys went ahead to saddle up." His face was grim.

"Are you feeling all right?"

"Of course I am," J.D. snapped.

Rachel had nothing else to say. When they reached the barn, Bluey gave her Rocky's reins. After tying on her slicker and putting her lunch in the saddlebag, she swung up into the saddle with more ease than she expected.

"I'm ready," she told J.D. again.

The other two men were on their horses.

"Follow me," J.D. said, and rode out of the barn into the cool, damp air.

Rachel did much the same job as she'd done yesterday, but today she knew what to expect. She didn't start out with the romantic attitude that she was on a lark. She knew she was going to work hard. But she also knew she could do it.

Around noon, J.D. dropped back beside her. "You ready to eat lunch?"

She was wearing her slicker again, with her braid tucked up under her hat. Looking at her watch, she realized a lot of time had passed. "I could eat. But I'm not sure I can ride and eat at the same time."

"How about a little hot coffee?"

"I'd kill for that," she admitted.

J.D. pulled out a thermos and poured some coffee into the lid, which served as a cup. He carefully handed it to Rachel.

"What about you and the others?" she asked.

"I'll take a drink after you, and Bluey has a thermos for him and Billy. I told him to drink all he wanted before he let Billy drink out of the same cup. I don't want Bluey to get sick."

"You think Billy's coming down with it?"

"Yeah, I do. He's not looking so good. But I think we'll finish up early, maybe around four. Would you like an early day? That will give me time to take care of the animals in the barn."

"I can help do that."

"No. You can soak in a tub and have a nap before dinner. Doesn't that sound better?"

"You know it does," she said with a smile, "but it hardly seems fair."

When she handed him the empty cup, he poured himself some coffee. "I appreciate your help more than I can say. But I know it's hard on you. I don't want you to do so much that you get sick again."

"I'm stronger than I look, J.D. And doing all these things I didn't know I could do makes me feel better about myself. Modeling for a living doesn't give me that feeling."

"So, after you leave here, you're going to want me to write you a reference letter?"

She grinned. "No, thank you. But if I wanted one, would you write me a good one?" She tilted her head and watched him carefully.

"I'd write you a wonderful letter, Rach. You're the best." With a smile, he put the thermos away and rode back to his position on the herd.

He'd never before used that shortened form of her name, like Rebecca did. It indicated a closeness Rachel wasn't sure she could trust, forced her to think about their relationship. She'd been so busy learning new things she'd almost forgotten why she'd been reluctant to see J.D. again. He'd made glorious love to her and then ridden away, out of her life.

Well, to be fair, she'd left, too. But she hadn't wanted to. He'd given her no encouragement to stay. And now he was calling her Rach.

"Rachel! Get that cow!" J.D. shouted.

Rachel awoke from her thoughts and chased after the cow, grateful for Rocky's skills. They got the animal back to the herd, and she reminded herself once again that this job did not lend itself to daydreaming.

When they reached the barn that evening, Rachel wasn't the one who couldn't get off her horse. She swung down, holding on to the saddle to be sure, but though her legs hurt, she could manage. It was Billy who still sat on his mount.

"J.D.?" she called, and hurried to Billy's side just in time to break his fall from his horse.

J.D. arrived in time to take most of his weight. "Let go, Rachel, I've got him now. I'll take him to the bunkhouse and get him some Tylenol and Gatorade. He'll feel better when I get him in bed."

"Yes, I'm sure he will. I'll help Bluey with the horses," she said, smiling at him.

He agreed with a nod and headed for the bunkhouse.

"Think it will be your turn tomorrow, Bluey?" Rachel asked.

"What do you mean?"

"Well, yesterday J.D. had to carry me in. Today he had to carry in Billy. I thought it might be your turn next."

"Mercy, I hope not. It would be humiliating."

While they chatted, she unsaddled her horse. Once she'd stored the gear, she did the same for Billy's horse, while Bluey took care of J.D.'s. Then they rubbed the horses down and fed them some oats.

"Ready for dinner now?" Bluey asked.

"Sure am. Now I know why you cowboys have such big appetites," she said with a grin.

"I reckon you do, Rachel. You've done a fine job for us."

"Think J.D. would hire me?"

"I doubt that. You'd be too much of a distraction on a regular basis. All the cowboys would be wanting to help you instead of doing their own jobs."

"So I guess I'll have to look for a job as housekeeper."

"You don't plan on going back to that modeling job you was doing?"

Who was she kidding? Of course she'd go back to modeling. After all, it was all she knew. She told Bluey that. "But I feel so useless when I do that job. Sometimes I think I need to change careers."

"Well, if I hear of any housekeeping jobs around, I'll be glad to let you know. And I'll tell them what a good cook you are. But I don't think you should try to get Madge's job."

Rachel stared at him. "Try to get Madge's job? Of

course not. She's the one who taught me everything, except riding, of course. I would never do that to Madge."

"Just wanted to be sure. She's a good woman. I wouldn't want her upset."

"Because you like her?" Rachel asked, watching him closely.

"A'course I like her." His cheeks were red.

"She likes you, too."

"We're all friendly on this ranch," Bluey said quickly, and held open the door for her to enter the warm, bright kitchen.

"We're back early, Madge," Rachel announced. "And Billy's sick."

"Oh, my. Here, have a cup of coffee. Dinner won't be ready for another half hour."

Rachel and Bluey sat down at the table. The hot coffee was a welcome treat.

"How did the day go?" Madge asked.

"It was fine," Bluey said. "We managed to get the herd in."

"Good. You know, Rachel, after you finish your coffee, you'll have time to take a shower before we eat." Then she turned back to the cowboy. "How are you feeling, Bluey?"

"I'm not getting sick, if that's what you're thinking," he said, stubbornness in his voice.

Madge reached out to touch his forehead. He almost fell out of his chair to avoid her hand.

"I was just going to see if you were running a fever, Bluey. You'd think I was attacking you," she protested, her voice huffy.

"Sorry, Madge, I'm not used to being touched. You can check now."

Madge reached out slowly to test his forehead.

Rachel looked away, feeling as if she was intruding in an intimate situation. She stood. "I'm going to take my shower." She hurried out of the room, hoping Bluey wasn't coming down with the flu, so that Madge could get closer to him.

Chapter Eleven

When Rachel came back to the kitchen, only Madge was there.

"While you were in the shower, your sister called."

"Which one?" Rachel asked, smiling because she had two sisters now.

"Rebecca. She wants you to call her. You should probably use the phone in the hallway in case J.D. or Bluey come in here and start talking," Madge said, but she avoided Rachel's gaze.

Rachel agreed, but she walked slowly, watching Madge over her shoulder.

When she dialed Rebecca's number, her nephew answered. "Hi, Aunt Rachel."

"Well, hi there, Joey. How are you?"

"I'm fine, but Mommy's not."

Rebecca frowned. "She's sick?"

"Sort of. She's in bed. I'll tell her you're on the phone."

Rachel held her breath until Rebecca picked up the telephone.

"Rebecca, what's wrong?"

"What do you mean?"

"Joey said you weren't feeling well."

"I have a little headache, that's all. Someday, when you're pregnant, you'll understand. You don't feel well for nine months."

"Ugh. Doesn't sound like fun."

"Well, the result is fun. Babies are wonderful."

"Do you know yet if it's a boy or a girl?"

"You're psychic!"

"I am?"

"I went to my doctor today. Or rather, Jeff and I went. We had the sonogram done, and I now have a picture of my baby girl."

"A girl? Oh, that's wonderful."

"Joey didn't think so."

"I hope you reminded him that Vivian is having a boy."

"I did. He's adjusting. He asked if everything would be pink. It seems he doesn't like pink."

"I don't think most males do. I'm so glad you're feeling all right."

"Are *you* feeling all right?"

"Yes. Becca, I can cook now, and I can ride a horse. I've been a regular cowboy the last couple of days!"

"Why? I thought you were trying to rest and get well."

"I'm well. I just need to put on weight. But we've had a flu epidemic here, and most of J.D.'s cowboys were out sick. Work doesn't stop on a ranch just because people get sick, so I offered to help out."

"You sound like you enjoyed it."

"I did. I mean, I was sore and very tired yesterday, but I did better today. And it makes me feel good to do something useful."

"When will you be coming home?"

"I don't know. Probably in a couple of weeks."

"You'll be here when Vivian has her baby, won't you?"

"I'll be there, I promise, but it's not due for two more months, right?"

"That's right, but the doctor said he might come early."

"I'm sure I'll be there in time, Becca. Okay?"

"Okay. But take care of yourself."

"I will. Bye," Rachel whispered, touched by her sister's concern. Rebecca and Vivian had both felt bad that, because of their pregnancies, Rachel couldn't stay with them. If J.D. hadn't offered to take her in, Rachel wasn't sure where she would've ended up.

When she came back to the kitchen, the others were just sitting down to dinner. She hurried to her chair.

"Was everything all right in Dallas?" Madge asked after they'd all been served and were eating.

"Oh, yes, fine. Becca called to tell me she's having a baby girl. They had the sonogram done this morning." Rachel beamed at the other three.

"She's happy about that?" J.D. asked.

"Oh, yes. She already has Joey. And Vivian is having a boy, so a little girl will be nice."

"Vivian's pregnant?" Bluey asked, shock on his face.

"Why, yes. I didn't know you knew Vivian."

"She and her husband used to come out once a year." A quizzical look crossed his weathered face. "But her husband is dead."

Rachel nodded. "About a year ago she married the private investigator she hired to find me and Rebecca and our brothers."

Bluey looked confused.

J.D. offered an explanation. "Rachel is Vanessa's blood sister. There were six of them, but when their parents died, they were split up. Rachel didn't even know she had a twin…or any siblings."

"Mercy, you do look like Vanessa, now that I think on it."

"Thank you, Bluey, that's a lovely compliment."

"And you have a twin?"

"Yes, we used to look exactly alike until I got so run-down and sick. And she's glowing right now because she's pregnant with her little girl."

J.D. laughed at Bluey's bewildered look. "It's a complicated family, Bluey, but it's good for Vanessa. Instead of it just being her and Vivian, she has a step-father, two sisters, two brothers, a nephew and a soon-to-be-born niece. Does that cover it, Rachel?"

"Yes, except that all our brothers aren't there." She sobered a bit. "One brother is dead, killed in Iraq. And Will, Vivian's husband, is still searching for our other brother, David. But he's found one brother. Jim is in the army serving in the Middle East. He's written us that he hopes to be back soon."

"Was Rebecca wanting you to come home?" J.D. asked, his smile gone.

"When I'm ready. She worries about me. And she's worrying about Vivian. She wants me home before Vivian has her baby."

"Why?" J.D. asked with a frown.

Rachel hesitated. "No one wants to say anything, but they're afraid something might be wrong."

"Why would they think that?" Madge asked, concerned.

"Well, the doctor says everything is okay but he's told them the baby might come early. And he's restricted Vivian's activities a lot." Rachel shrugged her shoulders. "She is forty-three, you know."

Bluey shook his head. "That seems young to me."

"It is young, Bluey, but not for her first pregnancy," Rachel said. "Women have babies at that age, but usually, they've been pregnant before."

After a moment, J.D. said, "If you need to get back, Rachel, you can go. We're not holding you here against your will."

She smiled at him. "Of course you're not. But I'm not ready to go back yet. I..." She searched for an excuse. "I need to put on a few pounds." It wasn't a totally lame excuse; nevertheless she had the feeling J.D. was looking right through her.

She wanted him to hold her here, all right. In his arms—and never let her go.

But, of course, that wasn't going to happen.

RACHEL WENT OUT with the cowboys again the next day. Two of the men had recovered, but J.D. didn't think they could last an entire day after being in bed for a week. He agreed that having Rachel there for one more day would make things go more smoothly.

She found herself riding quite comfortably, not tensing up, which made it easier. J.D. sent the two recovering cowboys in at noon. He, Bluey and Rachel continued working until about six o'clock again.

When they got to the barn, Rachel began unsaddling her horse.

"What are you doing?" J.D. demanded.

She stared at him. "Tending to my horse."

"I can do that. Go on up to the house."

She ignored him and pulled the saddle off Rocky. The weight almost bowled her over but she quickly found her balance, sure she could manage—until strong arms came around her and grabbed the saddle.

"Quit being so stubborn, Rach. You can go to the house now."

"J.D., I can take care of my horse. I know that's rule number one for cowboys. Your horse treats you well, and you return the favor."

"Who told you that? Was it Bluey?"

"No, I think you did. You were saying something about a cowboy. I think you were angry with him because he didn't take care of his horse."

"That doesn't apply to dudes," he muttered.

"I'm not a dude, am I, Bluey?"

"I reckon not, Rachel. You pulled your weight this week, but that don't mean J.D. can't take care of your horse."

"Not when I can do it. I couldn't the first day, but I did my horse and Billy's yesterday. I think I can take care of Rocky today."

"Okay, I'll let you take care of Rocky," J.D. said, finally relenting. "But may I put your saddle away? Or

do you insist on damaging your back trying to carry it?"
He gave her a superior grin.

"You can put away the saddle," Rachel agreed, but
she kept her chin in the air.

She removed Rocky's bridle and began rubbing her
down. Rachel found the rhythmic strokes to be sooth-
ing for the horse and for herself. She even found herself talking to Rocky. When her mount's ears twitched
and she swung her head around several times, Rachel
swore the horse even understood her.

When she'd finished and turned Rocky out into the
corral, Rachel walked into the house with Bluey and
J.D., feeling she'd done her share. "How's Billy?" she
asked.

J.D. replied, "I checked on him and the other two
who came out today. They're doing well as long as
they don't have to get out of bed."

"Poor dears," Madge said. "I'll go down after dinner and see if they need anything."

"I thought Cook was doing better," J.D. said.

"He is, but that doesn't mean he can take care of
everyone. That's a hard task," Madge assured him.

"I guess so."

"We'll clean the kitchen, Madge, so you don't have
to do that." Rachel looked around at the men, since
she'd included them in her offer, but they didn't protest.

"That would be nice. Are you sure you're doing all
right, Rachel?"

Before she could answer, J.D. spoke up. "She's
doing so well she insisted on taking care of her own
horse."

Rachel didn't remind him that it was the second day she'd taken care of Rocky. She was willing to let well enough alone.

Madge didn't comment. Instead, she got up from the table and headed to the storeroom. "All right, then. I'd better take some more supplies down there."

"Maybe I'd better carry things for you," Bluey said, getting up from the table. "Can you two manage here?"

Rachel and J.D. exchanged a look. Then he said to Bluey, "Yeah, we can manage, but wear one of those masks on your face when you go in."

"I will. I don't want to get sick."

When the pair left the kitchen, J.D. turned to Rachel. "Are they making any progress?"

Rachel knew what he meant. "I don't know. Madge tried to touch his forehead and you'd have thought she was going to hit him. He ducked back and almost fell over. When she explained what she was going to do, he told her to go ahead, that he wasn't used to being touched."

"I guess he isn't, come to think of it. None of us is unless we're, uh, in a relationship."

"Or have close family."

"I guess you're the only one of us who qualifies for that."

"That's not true. You have Madge. You kiss her on the cheek or give her a hug sometimes. She may not be a blood relative, but she's your family."

"I guess so." He shrugged. "Do you ever see your mother?"

"You mean the woman who adopted me?"

"Yeah. Who else would I mean?"

"Sorry. I don't think of her as my mother anymore. A real mother doesn't steal from her children."

J.D. pushed away from the table and stacked his dishes to take to the sink. "You sound a little bitter, Rachel."

"I am. I worked for ten years, saving my money for the future. I had no teenage years. I was too busy to go to proms, basketball games, or anything like that. And once I finished high school, college was out of the question. My mother made sure I was booked solid. She traveled with me as my personal assistant and drew a good salary out of what I made. Then she stole from me until I had nothing left."

"That's pretty rotten."

"Yes, it is. I haven't seen her in six months, ever since I found out what she'd done."

"Good thing you got a new family to replace her." He put his dishes in the dishwasher and turned to face her. "Are they perfect?"

"I'm sure they're not. Who is? In fact, Vivian is one of those mothers who may be too protective of her children. But she's so loving and forgiving, you can't hold it against her."

"Your mother wasn't loving?"

"No. She was cold and selfish."

"So why did you do what she told you?"

Rachel didn't answer until after she'd put her own dishes in the dishwasher. Then she turned to face J.D., leaning against the counter.

"I was still naive enough at fifteen to believe if I did

what she wanted me to do, it would please her and… she'd love me."

"You didn't think she loved you?"

She shook her head. "I guess you knew your parents loved you?"

"Yeah. How did you know yours didn't?"

"I don't even remember my father. He left when I was two, and she vilified him to me the rest of the time. You know, she never once told me she loved me." She gave a sarcastic laugh. "So I guess she didn't lie to me about that."

"Okay, so I understand why you love Vivian and Rebecca and Vanessa. I guess being away from them has been hard these last few weeks."

She nodded. "But even when I was staying at Vivian's, I was away a lot, working as much as I could so I'd have something for the future. Models don't have retirement funds, you know."

"Neither do ranchers," J.D. pointed out.

"At least I heard beef prices are up because of the mad cow disease."

"That's true. How did you know that?" he asked with a grin.

"I watched a lot of television the first week I was here. The soap operas didn't interest me, so I watched the news."

"And where did you learn the computer?"

"Oh, around. I took a basic course for a couple of weeks, and since then, I've taught myself. Do you have more data you want me to input?"

"You don't want to ride tomorrow?"

"Sure, but I wasn't sure you'd need me."

J.D. grinned. "I hate to admit it, but you're better than those half-sick cowboys who came out with us today."

Rachel gave a mock bow. "Why, thank you, kind sir. If you throw such lovely compliments at me, I'll insist on going."

"Just don't flirt with any of the men who ride out with us. Half of them have their eyes on you already."

"Only half?" she asked, giving him an arch look.

"I'm serious, Rachel. The work is dangerous if you don't concentrate on it. I don't want anyone hurt."

She sobered. "Neither do I."

"Good. So that's settled. I'll put a little extra in your paycheck this week, okay?" J.D. teased.

"I think my paycheck will have to go toward my bed and board. If there's any left over, it should go to Madge for doing double duty, tending the sick—first me and then the cowboys."

J.D. nodded. "Don't worry. I take good care of Madge."

"Good. I'm going to mop the floor now, so she won't have to do it."

"Okay. I'm going to go through the mail. I've been neglecting it for a few days."

He moved over to the computer desk, where a stack of envelopes was waiting for him.

Rachel got out the mop and began cleaning the floor. She hummed as she worked, feeling content in spite of the long day she'd had.

"You've got a nice voice," J.D. said, surprising her.

"What?"

"You were humming. It sounds good."

"I didn't mean to interrupt your work."

"You didn't." He smiled at her and turned back to his mail.

It suddenly occurred to her that she'd do almost anything for a smile like that. Not a good thought. She'd taught herself not to be so needy. Until she'd met J.D. Something about the man seemed irresistible.

The back door opened and Madge and Bluey came in.

"What are you doing, Rachel?" Madge demanded.

"I thought I could save you some work by mopping up. I'm just finishing."

"You are such a good person, child. Thank you. I was just telling Bluey I needed to get back and clean the floor."

"That's what she said," Bluey agreed.

"You'd better watch that romantic talk in the moonlight, Bluey, or she'll have you at the altar before you know it," J.D. said, which caused both Bluey and Madge to turn beet-red.

Rachel whirled around to glare at him. "J.D. Stanley, you are the most insensitive man I know!"

"What did I do?" J.D. asked, surprised by her attack.

"Oh, honestly. Just go to bed and leave them in peace!"

He stared at her and she tried to convey her meaning with her eyes. Finally, he stood. "Uh, yeah, I'm way too tired to do anything else tonight. I'm going to bed."

"Me, too," Rachel said. "I'm riding out again in the morning, so I'd better get some sleep."

She followed J.D. out into the hallway.

"Are you sure it's safe to leave them alone?" J.D. whispered.

"Yes, I think Madge is too old to get pregnant."

J.D. burst out laughing and Rachel shushed him. "Go to bed, J.D., before they figure out what we're doing."

"I'm not sure *I* know what we're doing."

"Just go to bed."

To her surprise, he leaned down and kissed her cheek. "I'll say thank-you for Madge, okay?"

Whatever it was he was trying to say was lost on her as soon as his lips touched her cheek. His kiss was featherlight, soft as a breeze, but her reaction was intense. Her heart sped up, her mouth went dry. She barely managed to choke out the words, "Okay, good night" as J.D. left her at her door.

Watching his back, she tried to get her pulse under control. *It was just a peck, Rachel,* she told herself. *What would you do if he really kissed you?*

She knew. She'd enjoyed J.D.'s kisses before.

And, God help her, she craved more.

Chapter Twelve

They had more cowboys riding out the next morning. So many, in fact, that Rachel had a partner riding drag. She thought that would be a good thing, but the man kept trying to impress her and do her work for her, so much that he drove her crazy.

She finally informed him that she could do her job and that he should concentrate on his.

"Aw, Rachel, I'm just trying to impress you."

"Please don't, Tony." She turned and rode back to the other side of the herd.

A loud cry startled her. She turned Rocky around to see Tony on the ground, his horse's reins hanging down. Then another sound caught her attention and she saw J.D. riding toward them, a scowl on his face.

She returned to where the cowboy lay on the ground. Swinging down from Rocky's back, she dropped her reins, knowing Rocky would stay there. Then she bent over Tony, the flirtatious cowboy.

"Are you all right?"

"I—I think I broke my arm," he gasped, clutching his right forearm.

J.D. knelt down beside Rachel. "What happened here?"

Tony didn't answer, so Rachel said, "I don't know. I was going in the other direction when I heard him cry out. He said he thinks he broke his arm."

J.D. looked at the man's arm and concurred with his diagnosis. "Yeah, I think you did."

Then he looked at Rachel. "I told you not to flirt with my men. It distracts them. No way would Tony have lost his grip if he'd been concentrating on his job." Without waiting for a response from her, he helped the cowboy to his feet. "Sorry, man, but you're going to have to ride back to the barn."

Then J.D. turned to Rachel once again. "Go tell Bluey he's in charge until I get back. I'd send you to the house except we're so shorthanded. Now go!"

Rachel went, but she wasn't a happy camper. Not only had she not flirted with Tony, she'd warned him to pay attention to his job.

And J.D. blamed her!

She explained to Bluey what had happened as the two of them rode in together that evening. He assured her he would tell J.D. what she'd said.

"Doesn't matter, Bluey. He won't believe me."

"He might. You seem to be able to persuade him to do things he'd never do on his own…like leave Madge and me alone last night."

Rachel's face brightened. "Did that work well for you?"

"Yeah. We're…in love," Bluey said self-consciously.

"Oh, Bluey, I'm so happy for you."

"I don't deserve her, you know. J.D. will probably talk her out of it."

"Over my dead body," Rachel said, gritting her teeth. "I know I shouldn't ask, but…are you going to get married?"

"If we can get J.D. on our side."

"But he shouldn't matter!" Rachel protested.

"He's the only family Madge has, except for her sister. She thinks of him as her son. I can't take her away from that."

"I understand," Rachel said, thinking about how hard life was. Madge had lost her husband and been alone for years. Now she'd fallen in love again, but it might cost her the one relationship she'd had for the last ten years.

Rachel was determined to help Madge out. Then she was going to pack her bags and head home. J.D. had convinced her, again, that there was no place in his life for her. The hopes that had been raised last night were once again dashed.

When she and Bluey reached the house, they found J.D. already sitting at the table.

He looked at Bluey as they came in. "Everything go okay?"

"Sure. Fine."

J.D. nodded to Rachel and then turned around.

Rachel walked straight through to her room. She grabbed a quick shower, not caring if she was late for dinner. But when she returned to the kitchen, Madge was still at the stove and the two men were talking. Frowning, Rachel walked to the housekeeper's side.

"Madge, is there anything—"

The woman fell to the floor.

Rachel knelt down beside her at once and realized she was running a high fever. Bluey and J.D. reached them before Rachel could say anything. Then she asked them to carry Madge to her room.

"What's wrong with her?" Bluey demanded anxiously.

Rachel put a reassuring hand on his arm. "She'll be okay in a couple of days. It's the flu. I'll get some Tylenol and Gatorade and be right there." She went to the storeroom but found only one small bottle of Gatorade. She called down to the bunkhouse, but they were about out, too, and they still had sick ones.

When Rachel got to the bedroom, she found Madge stretched out on the bed and the two men standing there, feeling useless.

"I'm going to put Madge to bed. But I need more Gatorade for her. And the men in the bunkhouse need some, too. Could you two go to Prairie View and get some for us?"

Relieved to have something to do, they rushed from the house.

Rachel tended to Madge, and the housekeeper was asleep by the time the men returned. They rushed in to find Rachel dishing up dinner. At the anxious look on Bluey's face, she announced, "You can go in and see how she's doing, Bluey. Dinner won't be on the table for about five more minutes."

The older cowboy sought J.D.'s approval. "Is that okay, J.D.?"

"Sure, it's fine."

Rachel turned her back on J.D., not wanting him to see the anger in her eyes. Bluey shouldn't have to beg J.D.'s permission to see Madge.

"Can I help you dish up dinner?" J.D. asked.

At the sound of his voice, she jumped. She hadn't heard him move, but he stood right behind her. "No, I'll manage."

He sat down at the table. "Bluey told me what happened today when Tony fell."

Rachel didn't respond. She had nothing to say.

"I guess I was a little hard on you. I'm sorry."

Those words made her turn around. "You guess?"

"Okay, Rachel, you didn't flirt with him. But you were a distraction. The men have been watching you ever since you got here. You don't look any less attractive on a horse, I can assure you."

"Oh, thanks," she said, her voice heavy with sarcasm.

He stared at her, but said nothing.

Rachel stepped around him and put a bowl of mashed potatoes on the table. "Did Bluey talk to you about him and Madge?"

"Yes, he did."

"Well?"

"Well, what?"

"Did you give them your blessing?"

"For what?"

"For them to marry!" Rachel glared at him.

J.D. frowned. "Bluey didn't say anything about that. Do they want to marry?"

"Yes, we do," Bluey said from the doorway. "I was trying to find a way to tell you this evening, but I was afraid you'd be upset with Madge."

"Damn it, Bluey, you've known me all my life. I'm not that unreasonable. I'm happy for you. You're not planning on taking her away, though, are you?" he asked, even as he stood to shake Bluey's hand.

Bluey grinned. "I couldn't take her away if I tried. She thinks of you like a son."

"I'm grateful. As Rachel said the other night, Madge is my family. But I'm glad to welcome you into it."

Rachel offered her congratulations and hugged Bluey, who still seemed uncomfortable. Then she put the rest of the meal on the table and they all sat down.

"I can't wait to tell Madge," Bluey said as he filled his plate.

"I'm sure she'll be excited," J.D. agreed.

Rachel passed around the food and said nothing. Though she was happy for the older couple, she couldn't help but think how her relationship with J.D. was such a mess.

J.D. looked at her. "Aren't you happy for Bluey and Madge?"

"Of course I am." She said nothing else, eating her meal as if she were dining alone.

J.D. frowned. Then he looked at Bluey, who shrugged his shoulders and shook his head.

After a quiet dinner, Bluey went back to check on

Madge. Rachel reminded him to wear a mask. She began clearing the dishes, and J.D. got up to help her.

"It's all right. I can manage." Her voice wasn't warm or friendly.

"What did I do to upset you?"

She didn't want to talk to him, but she was a reasonable woman.

"You still blame me for Tony's broken arm, even though you say you believe Bluey that I wasn't flirting with him."

"If he'd been working with another man, he would've been concentrating on his job."

"But doesn't that make it Tony's fault?"

J.D. sighed. "Yeah, but it doesn't change the fact that you being there caused it."

She grabbed the bowl he had in his hand. "Just get out of my kitchen and leave me alone," Rachel ordered, turning her back to him.

"Okay, fine. That's the reality of it, Rachel, whether you want to believe it or not."

He grabbed a couple of containers of Gatorade and stormed off for the bunkhouse.

Rachel hurried through the dishes. She didn't want to be there when J.D. came back. As soon as she had the kitchen cleaned up, she went to Madge's room to check on her patient.

"Hi, Madge. I didn't know you were awake. How are you feeling?"

The woman shook her head. "Not so good, I'm afraid."

"Well, there's some news that'll cheer you up. Did Bluey tell you that J.D. is happy about your marriage?"

Madge nodded and managed a smile.

Rachel turned to Bluey. "I think Madge needs to get to sleep now. Tomorrow's Sunday. I'll fix breakfast and you can take it in and enjoy it with her."

"Thanks, Rachel," Bluey said. "I'll just tell her good-night before I leave."

"Right. I'll see you both in the morning. Madge, if you need me during the night, just call."

As she left Madge's room, Rachel heard J.D. coming in the back. She hurried to her room and closed the door.

J.D. SAW RACHEL SCURRY away from him. She was obviously still angry with him. He sighed. He'd been honest with her. Clearly, he should've lied.

Bluey came out of Madge's room, saying good-night.

"Bluey, is Madge awake?"

"Sort of. You want to say good-night?"

"Yeah." He went to Madge's room. "Is there anything I can do for you?"

"No, Rachel took care of me. But you could put more boiling water in my hot-water bottle," Madge said, pulling it out from under the covers. "It really helps me fight off the chills."

"Sure. I'll be back in a couple of minutes."

Bluey came out with him. "I could do that, J.D., if you want to go on to bed."

"No way. I'm pleased to have something to do for her. Miss Perfect apparently did everything else."

"Are you talking about Rachel?"

"Yeah. I know, I know. I should be grateful for what she's done. And I am. But life was simpler before Rachel arrived on the scene."

"Are you talking about the first time or the second time?" Bluey asked calmly.

J.D. glared at him as he filled a kettle with water. "Take your pick. She causes turmoil wherever she goes."

"You're not being fair," the cowboy said.

"I know, but I'm just trying to survive."

"You might as well give in, J.D. I did, and it's much better."

"If I were guaranteed a happy ending, Bluey, I might give in, too. But Rachel's pretty mad at me right now."

"Yeah, she is."

When the water boiled, J.D. poured it into the rubber bottle. "I would never have thought of this."

"Me, neither. The cowboys didn't get this perk," Bluey said with a laugh.

"They have to be tougher, don't they?"

"Don't believe it, J.D. Women are a lot tougher than us. We have more muscles, but they do harder things."

J.D. looked at Bluey. When had this hardened cowboy turned into a sage? He clapped the older man on the back. "You may be right, Bluey."

RACHEL SET HER ALARM for 2:00 a.m. to check on Madge. When it went off, she slid out of bed and put on her robe, hoping the noise hadn't disturbed anyone. She hurried to Madge's room, finding her sleeping but feverish.

Rachel turned on the light in the kitchen to fetch the Tylenol. J.D. came stumbling into the kitchen, rubbing his eyes, much as he might have as a little boy. "Is something wrong?" he asked.

"I'm just getting some medication for Madge. There's nothing you can do. Go back to bed."

"Yeah, okay," he said, and turned away. He stumbled and Rachel thought he was going to fall. She reached out to him and discovered he, too, was burning up with fever. Suddenly he grabbed his mouth and turned, running for the bathroom.

"I'm sorry," he muttered a few moments later when he emerged. "Don't know what happened."

"I do," Rachel said wearily. "Come on. I'll help you back to bed. Then I'll bring you some medicine, too."

"You mean I've got the flu?"

He sounded so surprised, Rachel couldn't help but hug him. "Yes, J.D., you've got the flu. Come on back to bed." She led him to his big bed and tucked him in. He was shivering all over.

"I'll be right back. Try to stay awake, okay?"

First she took care of Madge, then went to J.D.'s room.

"J.D., are you still awake?"

He was shivering under the covers, but he nodded. She raised the blankets and slipped a hot-water bottle in against his stomach. Gradually the shivers subsided.

"J.D., don't go to sleep yet. I need you to swallow some Tylenol. Come on. Raise up on your elbow. Here we go," she said softly, helping him get the pills down.

"Thank you," he muttered, his eyes still closed.

Looking at him like this, she felt her anger subside. Not only was J.D. an incredibly handsome man, he could be gentle and sweet and boyishly charming and—

She stopped herself before she jumped into bed with him. Instead, she leaned over and kissed his forehead before she tucked him in again. "Sleep tight, J.D., I'll see you in the morning."

Chapter Thirteen

"I've got to go to work."

Rachel looked up from her breakfast to see J.D. standing in the kitchen doorway. A very sick-looking J.D. She motioned to Bluey, who dropped his fork atop his stack of pancakes the moment he saw his boss.

"No, J.D., it's Sunday," he said. "There's no work."

"And no church, either," Rachel added. "You're sick with the flu. You need to be back in bed."

He held his arm up as if to hold her off as she rose from her chair. "No, I…" He never finished the words, but started to sway. Rachel and Bluey ran and braced each side of the big man. He was sinking fast.

"But my breakfast…"

Leave it to a cowboy to want food, Rachel thought. "If you're hungry, I'll bring you some plain pancakes, but you've got to get back to bed."

Bluey gripped him around the waist and assisted him out of the kitchen.

In no time Rachel had a plate of pancakes and some Gatorade on a tray, and was heading to J.D.'s room. She was grateful that Bluey had looked in on Madge earlier and taken care of her.

Once she reached J.D.'s bedroom, she moved a chair beside his bed. She didn't want to sit on the bed with him. That was too intimate. She looked down at him and noticed his eyes were closed. "J.D., are you awake?"

He muttered something.

Against her better judgment she used the opportunity to stare at him. His wavy brown hair dipped over his forehead like melting chocolate, and she fought the urge to wipe it away. His jaw was strong and sculpted, the perfect frame for perfectly shaped lips. How well she remembered how they felt against hers, hot, firm, soft. She looked down at the column of his neck and further…but the sheet blocked her view. Tempted though she was, she resisted pulling it down and feasting her eyes on his body.

She was here to feed the man. Nothing else.

"I have your breakfast, J.D. Open your mouth and I'll give you a bite."

To her surprise he followed her orders, but he didn't open his eyes. She slipped in a bite, and as soon as he tasted it, he looked at her. "That's good," he said faintly.

Her heart nearly stopped when she caught sight of his tongue peeking out to swipe at an errant crumb on his lower lip. That tongue had done such wonderful things to her—

"I—I'm glad you like it," she said, stirring herself from her erotic reverie. She gave him another bite, then offered him a drink. To help him, she wrapped an arm around his neck and raised his head, feeling the heat coming off his body. She figured by now her own body temperature was probably just as scorching.

After he'd eaten a few more bites, she told him to rest, that he'd probably had enough. Being so near him, touching him, looking at him in his bed—it was too much for her.

In the seconds it took her to move the chair and grab her tray, he'd fallen back asleep.

She knew it was a mistake, but she leaned over and kissed him. just on the forehead.

"Love you, too," he muttered. Or at least she thought that was what he said.

As much as she wanted to believe he was talking to her, she figured he was delirious with fever and had no idea who she was. Probably Madge.

But a girl could dream, couldn't she?

When she entered the kitchen she walked straight to the sink. Not to wash her hands of germs, but to sprinkle cold water on her face and neck. It was the closest she was getting to the proverbial cold shower.

Did she have it that bad? she asked herself. The man was sick and she was panting over him….

Before she started to talk to herself, she noticed Bluey nursing a cup of coffee at the table.

"How'd he do?" he asked.

"Surprisingly well. But we'll see if he can keep it down."

He gave her a crooked grin. "Be a right shame if he lost those delicious pancakes. You know I can't hardly believe you didn't know much about cookin' before you got here."

"Thanks, but it's all Madge's doing. She's a wonderful teacher. Even if I messed up, she made me feel good about my effort."

"Yeah, that's Madge. She demands a lot of herself but she forgives everyone else."

Rachel smiled. "Good quality in a wife, wouldn't you say?"

Bluey laughed and agreed. Then he pushed back his chair. "Much as I'd like to sit and shoot the breeze with you, I've got men to see to down at the bunkhouse."

"And I've got chores to do." As Bluey left the house, Rachel began tackling her to-do list. The morning passed quickly, with a few time-outs from her duties to check on her two patients.

By the time they both awoke, it was noon. She helped Madge change into a fresh nightgown and assisted her out of bed and into a comfortable chair in the den.

Since Bluey wasn't back yet, she took clean underwear into J.D.'s room.

"I thought you'd like to change," she said in an unfamiliar voice. "You know, get out of your sweaty clothes." Her mind was in overdrive, already envisioning stripping off his T-shirt and revealing his naked chest.

With what looked like all the strength he could muster, J.D. reached out and yanked the clean laundry from her hands, leaving her feeling cheated. "I can manage," he said hoarsely.

Rachel nodded and left the room, standing in the hall outside his door, waiting and listening. When he hadn't come out in five minutes, she knocked. "Are you all right?"

"I'll be right out."

When he opened the door a moment later, she had a big robe waiting for him, one she'd dug out of his closet. She'd bet he hadn't worn it in years, if ever, judging by the look on his face.

"What's this?" he asked.

"A robe. I want you to go sit in a soft chair in the den while I make your bed."

"You don't need to do that," he managed to say.

"It'll make you feel better to lie down later on clean linens," she said as she helped him put on the robe over a pair of sweatpants. "Besides, Madge and Bluey are waiting for you to watch the game with them." She'd heard Bluey come in a moment ago and turn on a Texas Rangers game. She knew that would get J.D. to cooperate; he loved baseball.

After she settled him in the den and got them each a bowl of soup she'd made earlier, she figured she'd tackle the linens, but J.D. had other plans.

"Sit with us. You have to eat."

By now Rachel needed to put distance between her and J.D. She'd spent entirely too much time being too close to him this morning, and her heart was paying the price. But when Madge and Bluey insisted, too, she had no choice. She got her own bowl of soup and took a seat on the opposite side of the sofa. As she watched the game—or rather watched J.D. watch the game—she couldn't recall the last time she'd enjoyed a sporting event more.

She looked around the room and couldn't stop her mind from racing. If she ignored reality, she could almost believe she belonged here, at the ranch, with J.D. Unlike when she'd first arrived, she now could envision herself living in West Texas as a rancher's wife. It was a far cry from modeling, but a good alternative. Here she felt like she actually made a difference.

After J.D.'s rudeness toward her about Tony's accident, she'd thought she would be leaving. Instead, here she was, staying for another week at least, until Madge was well. But it was no sentence. Rachel relished her time here. Perhaps too much. After all, it had to come to an end sometime.

She hoisted herself off the sofa and made up J.D.'s and Madge's beds. When she returned to the den, she told Bluey, "It's time to get these guys back to bed. We don't want them to overdo it."

Once they had the patients settled in their rooms, Rachel ambled into the kitchen to wash their bowls and figure out what to make for dinner. As she was looking through Madge's recipes, Bluey came in.

"I can't believe you made my bed and did my laundry. Rachel, you're trying to do too much," he declared.

She smiled at him. "I'm just trying to accomplish what Madge does every day."

"She is amazing, isn't she?" he agreed.

Rachel thought his partiality toward Madge was so romantic. If she ever had anyone who loved her as Bluey loved Madge, she knew she'd be very happy.

But obviously that wasn't in the cards for her. At least not with J.D. Stanley.

She smiled at Bluey. "Yes, she is, and you're a lucky man." She turned her attention back to the recipes. "I thought I'd make this pasta dish tonight. It's plain enough for J.D. and Madge to eat."

Bluey agreed and they worked on the casserole together. In short order they were done. "Look at that," he remarked. "We still have time for a game of gin rummy."

"You play gin?" Rachel asked, surprised.

"Sure do. We play in the bunkhouse for high stakes. But you and I'll play for who does the dishes after dinner."

"Gladly," she said with a laugh.

Playing cards was exactly the kind of activity that relieved Rachel's tension and got her mind off her situation. The game was even until they got close to the end. Then Bluey made a circumspect move.

"Bluey, you fake! You lost on purpose!"

He feigned an innocent look. "You don't think I *like* to do dishes, do you?"

Rachel had to laugh at his expression. "How 'bout we do them together?"

"You're on." Bluey stacked the cards and put them away so they could set the table. But first he went to check on J.D. and Madge.

Rachel sat at the table, thinking about how much she'd miss this kitchen and Madge and Bluey. She'd even miss J.D., though she'd trained herself not to think about him. At least she had after her first visit to the ranch.

She'd have to start all over again once she left again.

And it would be more difficult. Last time, she'd spent only three days with J.D. on the ranch. Now she'd spent weeks here. She'd learned to ride and to cook. A sadness invaded her as she faced the future.

"They're still sleeping," Bluey announced as he entered the kitchen, drawing Rachel from her depressing thoughts.

"Oh, good."

"Is anything wrong, Rachel?" he asked.

"No, of course not. How's the weather outside? And how many cowboys are going to ride out tomorrow?"

"Six plus me. We're almost back to normal. And there's no rain in the forecast. You rode under the worst circumstances, Rachel, and you never complained at all. I was impressed."

"I complained…about J.D. He sort of apologized, but he still said Tony's accident was my fault."

"Did you ever think that he can't get past how attractive you are because he's so attracted to you?" Bluey asked with a grin.

"Nice try, Bluey, but he's always made it clear he's not interested in me. At least not permanently."

"But, Rachel—" Bluey began. However, he was immediately distracted by Madge's voice.

"Madge is awake," he announced as he ran from the kitchen.

Rachel smiled at his devotion. Madge was a lucky woman.

She went to check on J.D. because she had nothing else to do, but he was still sleeping. Rachel quietly closed his door and moved to Madge's room, where she heard her and Bluey whispering quietly to each other. Rachel didn't want to intrude so she headed back to the kitchen.

Bluey returned shortly. "Madge thinks she's strong enough to come to the table. She wants you to help her with her robe."

"Are you sure, Bluey? We don't want her to overdo it."

"You go argue with her. I can't change her mind."

She left Bluey grinning in the kitchen and went to Madge's room. "Are you sure you should get up?" she asked.

"Just for a little while. I think it's because I've been able to keep things down. It makes me stronger."

"I hope so. Okay, for a little while. But the minute you start feeling bad, you let us know and we'll get you back to bed." Rachel helped Madge into her robe and kept her arm around her until she got her to a chair at the table.

"I don't know where Bluey went. He was here when I—"

They both turned to look at the door to the hallway when they heard noises. Bluey came into view with J.D. leaning on his shoulder.

"I guess it's time to serve dinner," Rachel said. She pulled out the casserole that she'd left in the warm oven and set it on hot pads on the table. Then she put rolls in the oven to heat.

In minutes they'd all sat down to eat together.

"Smells good," J.D. said, casting her a sincere look.

As they ate, Rachel and Bluey kept a close eye on

their patients. When they heard a knock on the back door, Bluey and Rachel exchanged a quick look. She pushed back her chair. "I'll see who it is."

She walked through the porch to the door and opened it to see a young blond woman dressed in tight jeans and an even tighter T-shirt.

"Yes?"

"Who are you?" the woman snapped.

"What can I help you with?" Rachel asked with determination.

"I'm here to see J.D., of course!"

"I'm afraid he isn't feeling too well. If you'll give me your name, I'll have him call you when he's better."

"I wouldn't worry about that. He'll want to see me."

"No, he won't. He's sick."

"He'll want to see me," the woman said insistently. "After all, he's my fiancé."

Chapter Fourteen

Rachel stared at the young woman, in momentary shock. Then her manners kicked in. She stepped back and waved her hand. "Come in."

The woman followed her to the kitchen.

Since Rachel didn't know her name, she said, "J.D.'s fiancée is here."

"What?" Bluey asked in surprise.

"No, she's—" Madge never finished what she intended to say because she made a mad dash to the bathroom.

As if he finally realized what Rachel had said, J.D. opened his mouth to speak, but instead followed Madge.

Rachel and Bluey helped them back to their beds. After J.D. was settled, Rachel came back to the kitchen to find the so-called fiancée still waiting. The blonde hadn't moved. She stood in the kitchen with an annoyed look on her face, as if angry that she'd been abandoned. Her makeup was flawless, and Rachel decided this woman could be a model herself.

She believed the woman had lied about being J.D.'s

fiancée, but she wasn't going to call her on it. Things could be straightened out later—between her and J.D.

Instead, she said, "I trust you believe me now when I say that J.D. is sick and can't deal with visitors at present—even his fiancée." She put her hands on her hips and stared at the guest.

"Well, tell him I came to see him."

"Of course. Unfortunately, I don't know your name."

"J.D. will know," she said, her tone taunting.

Rachel followed her out on the porch, wanting to make sure she left. Just as they reached the door, the visitor turned and looked at her again. In a sneering voice, she said, "You never said who *you* are."

Rachel was in a feisty mood. She stared at the young woman and then said, "Oh, I'm his *other* fiancée!" Then she closed the door in the blonde's shocked face.

"I'll pay for that," she muttered to herself, "but I enjoyed saying it, anyway."

Bluey was in the kitchen again. "You talking to yourself?"

"Yes, I was, Bluey. Does that mean I'm going crazy?"

He shook his head. "I hope not, 'cause I do it, too. Did Stacy leave?"

"Is that her name? She never introduced herself other than to say she's J.D.'s fiancée."

Bluey grinned. "She wishes. She's been chasing after J.D. for a year. He took her out a few times, but then, about the time you came, he wouldn't have anything to do with her anymore."

Rachel would have liked to read into Bluey's words

that J.D. had remained faithful to her. But that was ridiculous. They parted without any commitments and hadn't spoken to each other for six months. More than likely he must have just gotten fed up with Stacy.

"What did she say to you before she left?" Bluey asked.

"Not much. I just got her out of the house and shut the door. She'll probably complain to J.D. the next time she talks to him."

"Don't worry about it. He'll be glad she's gone."

But Rachel couldn't help wondering how he'd feel when he learned about her final remark to Stacy.

BY THE END OF THE WEEK, Madge was doing much better. J.D., on the other hand, was not improving. He slept through his days, and when he did wake up, he was grumpy and confused. Rachel had never been around a worse patient.

After one session with him, Madge told Rachel she had more patience than a saint.

"No, Madge, I understand his frustration. I felt that way when I came down with pneumonia."

"You didn't show it, child. You were a wonderful patient."

"But I had you as my nurse."

"Maybe I can start helping with J.D. tomorrow. I'm feeling better every day."

Since Madge still took frequent naps and hadn't resumed any of her duties, Rachel said, "We'll see. Bluey would kill me if I let you have a relapse."

"Isn't he wonderful?" Madge asked.

Rachel smiled at her. "He's the best. He's been terrific, helping me here while he's working every day. He may be tired when he comes in, but he spends all his evenings checking on you or offering to help me. I don't know what I would've done without him."

Madge had a dreamy look in her eyes as she nodded in agreement. Then she suddenly sat up straight, clutching her coffee mug. "Bluey said Stacy came here claiming to be J.D.'s fiancée. You didn't believe her, did you?"

"Bluey explained everything. It's fine, Madge. Even if J.D. is engaged to her, it's none of my business." She tried to make sure she said those words with no emotion. But it was hard. As much as she resisted, she could feel her spine straighten involuntarily. Stacy hadn't been back and that was just fine with her.

Madge opened her mouth to protest, but they both heard J.D. calling. "I'd better go," Madge said, getting up and heading for J.D.'s bedroom.

Rachel remained where she was, knowing she had to start withdrawing emotionally if she was going to survive her remaining time on the ranch. Truthfully, she didn't want to withdraw. It surprised her, but she'd discovered that she loved life out here. Even more importantly, she'd discovered that she loved J.D. But that wasn't a surprise. She'd been in love with him ever since her first trip to the ranch. She hadn't realized how much until after she'd mishandled that last encounter and gone away. Now she didn't think J.D. would give her another chance.

Not that she blamed him.

But it was what she wanted more than anything in the world. She'd known that the moment she'd opened Vivian's door to him back in Highland Park.

"J.D.'s hungry." Madge's voice broke into her thoughts. Futile thoughts, she told herself. There could be no future for her and J.D. The sooner she realized that, the better.

She forced a weak smile. "That's a good sign. I'll heat him up some soup."

"I'll go keep him company until you bring it in," Madge said, already on her way to his room. "Maybe I can get him to drink a little more."

"Thanks, Madge."

Rachel was grateful for the help, really she was. Up till now she'd been the one feeding J.D. She'd treasured those few minutes by his bed, but she had to let Madge take over. She imagined J.D. would like it that way. And it would protect her heart.

WHEN MADGE ENTERED his room again, J.D. swallowed his disappointment. "Where's Rachel?" he asked, trying to keep his voice casual.

"She's fixing your lunch. I'm going to feed you, though. She's worked so hard, taking care of the both of us, and I'm still not able to do much. We owe her a lot."

"She's not getting sick, is she?" he asked anxiously.

"Not so far. She and Bluey are the only ones who have remained upright. By the way, Bluey says we're back to full strength except for you and me."

"We owe Bluey a lot, too. I'll make sure I put a

good bonus in his paycheck this month. He can spend it on your honeymoon."

"Don't be ridiculous!" Madge protested. "We're too old for such things as honeymoons."

"You're going to turn down my gift?"

"What are you talking about?"

"I've been doing some thinking, when I'm not sleeping. I want to give you and Bluey a honeymoon as your wedding present. Wherever you want to go."

"J.D., you can't do that! It would cost too much."

"Think of it as a bribe, Madge. I want you and Bluey to come back. I can't manage without either of you."

"Mercy, child, we're coming back. We'll look for a place to live nearby and—"

"What's wrong with here? Hell, we've got six bedrooms. That's not enough room for you?"

"Well, of course there's enough room. But we didn't know if you'd want us here."

J.D. closed his eyes, relaxing against his pillow. "Yes, I want you here, Madge. You're my family, and I think family should stick together. Will Bluey mind?"

"I don't think so. He's moving back to the bunkhouse to make sure there isn't any talk about us, you know, anticipating our wedding vows, but he liked being up here the past week or so."

"Well, you talk with him about it. Choose whatever rooms you want. You take two rooms and make one of them your sitting room, so you two can be alone in the evenings, if you want."

"That's very generous of you, J.D."

Rachel entered with his lunch tray. "What's J.D. being generous about?" she asked.

"He's invited me and Bluey to live here."

"Good. I'm glad to see he's thinking coherently."

"When didn't I?" he demanded, trying to sit up. He hated looking so weak in front of Rachel.

"I don't know," she said with a shrug. "Maybe the night your fiancée came calling."

J.D. almost fell out of bed. "When what?" he demanded in stern tones.

Madge decided she should explain. "It was when we were both pretty much out of it. Stacy turned up and wanted to see you. Rachel told her you were sick, but she said she was your fiancée and you would want to see her."

"Did anyone get around to telling you she's not my fiancée?" J.D. demanded, staring at Rachel. He was careful not to let too much emotion show, or they'd suspect his feelings for Rachel. If he had the strength he'd go tell that Stacy what he thought of her antics. Couldn't she take a hint? He'd told her bluntly that their relationship was over—not that they'd ever had one, really. He hoped Bluey had explained that to Rachel.

"Yes, don't worry about it," Rachel assured him, but she avoided his gaze, and he knew there was something she wasn't telling him. But he wasn't going to grill her in front of Madge. Besides, he didn't have enough energy yet to do so. Maybe after he had lunch and a nap.

"Let me know if you need anything else, Madge," Rachel said, and turned to leave. Then she looked back at J.D. "Enjoy your lunch, J.D."

"Thanks," he muttered, his gaze glued to the door where she disappeared.

"Lunch, J.D.," Madge called out to him. "Come on, pay attention."

It wasn't easy when his mind was on one feisty brunette who seemed hell-bent on avoiding him.

BLUEY TOLD MADGE that now that he was sleeping in the bunkhouse again, he should eat dinner there, too.

She protested at once. "I don't see why. You eat breakfast with them. I think I deserve your company during dinner. I don't get to see much of you anymore."

"I'll take it as a personal insult," Rachel added. "I don't think my cooking is that bad."

Bluey got completely flustered. "Madge, I can't— Rachel, of course you can— I mean— You're being unfair!" he finally said.

Rachel took pity on him. "I was just teasing, Bluey."

"Well, I wasn't," Madge said. "We've got plans to make. It much easier to discuss things while we're eating. Rachel always has good ideas, and J.D. has to be consulted on some things."

"She has a point," Rachel said, trying to be supportive.

"I guess so," Bluey agreed. "I can tell the boys that. They'll understand, then."

"You have to explain to them?" Madge questioned, showing her irritation.

"Madge, he's under peer pressure. It's tough," Rachel said, this time supporting Bluey, now that Madge had gained her point.

"That's right. They rib me enough as it is," Bluey added.

He immediately had Madge's sympathy. "Oh, sweetheart, I'm sorry. I didn't know."

Rachel knew Madge would've flown into his arms if she hadn't been there. Which made her feel like a fifth wheel. "I'll, uh, I'll go check on J.D. He might want to get up for dinner." She hurried out of the kitchen. When she returned, she'd be sure to cough or make noise so she didn't embarrass them again.

She looked in on J.D., as she'd said, but he was sleeping. With nothing else to do, she went to her bedroom. She had about fifteen minutes before she needed to return to the kitchen. As she sat there, she noted the various things in her room that told a story. The boots she'd bought so she could be a "cowgirl." The hat Madge had loaned her while she rode for J.D. The jeans she'd bought because that was the most practical gear on a ranch.

Actions spoke louder than words, she realized. She'd been preparing for life on a ranch. It didn't make sense. She knew she'd be going back to the city, back to the job she considered useless except for a way to earn some money.

She knew it, but she didn't want to accept it.

"Good thing J.D. can't see what I'm seeing," she muttered.

She got up and put her boots in the back of the closet, stowed away her jeans and vowed to return the cowboy hat to Madge. That would keep her mind off what she wanted.

And what J.D. didn't want.

After all, she thought sarcastically, if she stayed, the cowboys might get distracted! Heaven forbid they should learn some self-discipline.

With a sigh, she stood to go back to the kitchen.

"Rachel?" J.D. called.

She hurried to his room. His eyes were barely open. "Yes, J.D.?"

"Is it suppertime?"

"Almost. Are you hungry?"

"Yes. I want out of this damn bed. Maybe you'd better send Bluey in here. That way I can spare your blushes."

"I don't remember blushing," she told him, but she did as he asked. It was a good way to announce her return to the kitchen, too. "Bluey? J.D. needs your help."

As he came out of the kitchen, she said, "That's another reason you should be here in the evenings. J.D. still needs you."

"Good thinking, Rachel. I guess I have enough reasons to stay. Thanks."

Rachel went back into the kitchen with a smile on her face. She repeated her words to Madge and received praise in return.

"You can thank J.D.," Rachel said. "He asked for Bluey. He said to spare my blushes, but I think it was to spare *his*."

"I'm sure you're right. He doesn't remember the first few days of his illness, and that's a good thing."

"Yes, it is."

Rachel got busy with dinner, trying to forget about

J.D., but she immediately began thinking of ways to make the food look more attractive to him.

J.D. managed to eat more than he had in days. Rachel even offered him dessert. "Do you think you could eat any peach cobbler?"

"Maybe just a little bit," he said. "It's one of my favorites."

She set a bowl of warm cobbler down in front of him and couldn't resist patting his shoulder. When their gazes met, however, she hurried back to the stove.

Madge broke the awkward silence. "You know, Rachel, I believe you make cobbler better than me. You have such a light hand with the pastry."

Rachel laughed. "Madge, I'll believe most of your praise, because I want to, but even I can't believe that remark."

"True," Bluey said. "Madge is the queen of light pastry."

Madge blushed. "But Rachel's is very good," she protested.

J.D. nodded. "No one's arguing that, Madge. I don't know what we would've done without her this past week or two."

"I've enjoyed it," Rachel said.

When the other three laughed, she said, "It's true. I've learned so much here, but this week I've proved to myself I could really do it without Madge helping me. It's like scoring an *A* on a final exam, when you weren't sure you could do it."

"I think you scored an *A-plus,* Rachel, and we're grateful," J.D. said quietly.

His sincerity pleased her more than his words. "Thank you."

Their conversation turned to Madge and Bluey's honeymoon plans.

"Have you decided where you want to go?" J.D. asked.

The two exchanged a look before Madge answered. "Well, if it's not too much to ask, we'd like to spend the week in San Antonio in a hotel on the River Walk. That looks so romantic to me, and Bluey said he'd like it, too."

J.D. laughed. "Madge, from the way you began your request, I thought you were going to ask for a grand tour of Europe. Of course you can go to San Antonio."

"Europe? I'd never ask for that!"

"I thought you might have a hankering to see the Eiffel Tower or Big Ben," J.D. teased. "Are you sure that's what you want? You could go to the Bahamas, New York City, wherever you want."

"We want San Antonio," she said firmly. "We'll feel comfortable there and can relax and enjoy ourselves."

"Good enough. I'll start making arrangements as soon as you set a date."

"Well," Bluey said in an apologetic tone, "we'd like it to be soon. We don't have as much time left as a young couple would, and we want to spend it together."

"And," Madge added, "we want to have Rachel at our wedding."

"I'll be there whenever it is, Madge, I promise." Rachel couldn't imagine not being at their wedding.

Madge extended her hand across the table. "You're

more like my daughter than a stranger, Rachel. I'm so glad you'll come."

"But it would be easier to have the wedding before she leaves," Bluey said. "We don't want nothing fancy."

"I want to do you both proud," J.D. protested.

"Maybe we could do both, J.D.," Rachel said slowly. "As pretty as the weather is now, we could set up a trellis outdoors and decorate it with fresh flowers. The pastor could stand there and perform the marriage ceremony, with everyone sitting in folding chairs.

"Then, afterward, we could have a wedding cake and hors d'oeuvres and champagne if you want. And a bowl of punch. I think it would be lovely. Everyone could mix and mingle and enjoy themselves."

"Oh, that sounds like exactly what I'd want," Madge said, a big smile on her face.

"Me, too," Bluey agreed.

"It would be a lot of work," J.D. warned Rachel.

"I'd love doing it," she assured him.

"Okay," he stated. "You two decide on a date and we'll put everything in motion."

"Maybe we'd better have our discussion in private," Madge said. "We'll go into the den, so you two can enjoy your coffee, though, J.D., you shouldn't drink too much of it."

"Hey, I'm still working on my dessert."

J.D. watched them as they left the room hand in hand. "It's kind of sweet, isn't it?"

"Yes. And I think your offer of a honeymoon trip is wonderful, J.D."

"I was prepared to spend a lot more than a trip to San

Antonio will cost me." He grinned. "Maybe I can throw in a few extras."

"That would be nice," she agreed. As she started to stand, J.D. caught her wrist.

"Wait a minute. I wanted to ask you something."

"What?" she asked, her tone cautious.

"When you were telling me about Stacy coming here, it seemed to me that you didn't tell me everything. Is there something else, something she said?"

Rachel pulled her wrist from his hold and stood, stacking dishes. "Well, there is something… Not something she said, though."

She put the dishes in the sink and turned to face J.D. as he sipped on his coffee.

"I'm afraid I lost my temper." She shrugged her shoulders. "I didn't mean to cause problems, but she was being so—so difficult that when she demanded to know who I was, I—I told her I was your *other* fiancée."

J.D. choked and spewed his coffee all over the table.

Chapter Fifteen

Madge and Bluey settled on a date two weeks away.

Rachel felt she must've influenced them, since she was pleased to have that much longer on the ranch. However, life suddenly became much busier as Madge returned to her duties a little at a time, and the two of them started planning the reception.

J.D. finally went back to work, which gave them more time, but Rachel had to admit she missed his presence.

She and Madge were working at the kitchen table when the phone rang a couple of afternoons later. Madge answered the phone but, focused as she was on wedding details, Rachel didn't realize anything was wrong until something in Madge's voice caught her attention.

"Yes. Yes, of course. I'll find a way. No, don't worry. Everything will be fine. I'll let you know when I'll get there."

Madge hung up the phone and covered her face with her hands.

Rachel sprang up from her chair and put her arms around her. "What is it? What's wrong?"

"My sister fell and broke her hip. She was crying on the phone. They're doing hip replacement surgery tomorrow. She'll be in the hospital for two or three days afterward. Then she can go home if she has someone to take care of her. I've got to go to Dallas."

"Oh." Rachel realized immediately what was wrong in addition to her sister's accident. "The wedding!"

"Yes. I hope J.D. hasn't made any travel arrangements yet. And, Rachel, can you stay and fill in for me?"

She'd thought she had less than a week left at the ranch. But now she'd be here much longer. Happiness and regret warred within her. "Of course I can, Madge. I know you have to go to your sister. It's a shame about the wedding, though."

"Yes, it certainly is. I hope Bluey will understand. Oh, dear, what if he doesn't? What if he breaks our engagement because he doesn't want to wait? What am I going to do?"

"Madge, you know Bluey better than that. Go start packing. Everything will work out."

As soon as Madge left the room, Rachel grabbed the walkie-talkie. She hadn't used it before, but she was going to give it a shot. "J.D., this is base, come in."

"Rachel? Is something wrong?"

"Yes. Madge's sister is in the hospital. She really needs to talk to Bluey if you can spare him. It would help her a lot."

"We'll be right there."

Rachel was surprised that J.D. was coming, too, but maybe they were working close to the barn. She cleared away the papers from the table and put on a fresh pot of coffee.

She hoped she'd done the right thing, but she didn't want Madge to suffer more than she had to. It was bad enough that she had to leave Bluey and postpone her marriage without thinking he would understand. Rachel felt sure Madge was shedding a few tears as she packed.

The two men came hurrying into the house. Rachel sent Bluey to Madge's bedroom and told J.D. to sit down. She put a cup of coffee and a piece of chocolate cake in from of him as she filled him in. "I was afraid you'd think I was being melodramatic, but Madge sounded so miserable."

"No, I'm glad you called. Does she want to get there before the surgery?"

"I really don't know, but I'd think so. That will mean driving in tonight, and I'm not sure that's a good idea, as upset as she is."

"No, it's not." He got up and walked to the kitchen door. "Madge, Bluey, can you come in here? We need to discuss the details."

He sat back down, eating his cake, waiting. When a teary-eyed Madge came in with Bluey, J.D. stood up and hugged her. "I'm sorry about your sister. How old is she?"

"She's sixty-six, but she doesn't take care of herself. I've told her to, but she doesn't listen."

"Well, look, I don't think you should drive tonight."

"But the surgery is early in the morning, and I told her I'd see her before that," Madge said, her tone urgent.

"You can do so. I'm going to hire a plane to fly you into Dallas Love Field tonight. You can take a taxi to your sister's house. Do you have a house key?"

"Yes, she gave me one."

"Can you borrow her car?"

"Oh, I hadn't thought of that. Yes, I know where the duplicate key is. Oh, thank you, J.D. That will simplify everything. Rachel promised to take care of y'all."

"Rachel, if you need to go back—" J.D. began.

Did he want her to leave? She couldn't tell from his facial expression. Still, she'd made a promise to Madge. "No, no, I'm fine with it. More practice for me," she hurriedly assured him, not wanting to be sent away.

"Great. Okay." He looked at his watch. "Can you be ready to leave in an hour?" he asked Madge.

"Yes," she agreed, throwing Bluey a longing look.

"I'll take her to the airport," Bluey immediately said. There was a small county airstrip not far away.

"Do you want to go with her, Bluey?" J.D. asked.

"I'd like to, but I'd just be in the way. It's better that I stay here and work, since I'll be taking a week off for our honeymoon, whenever it is."

Madge bravely nodded in agreement.

"Okay," J.D. stated. "I'll go make the arrangements." He left the kitchen, heading for the den.

"Madge, is there anything I can help you do?" Rachel asked.

"No, dear, I'm fine. I'm almost finished packing."

"Why don't you sit down and have a piece of cake and coffee. I think sugar is good for shock."

She cut two pieces of cake and poured them coffee.

Then she left them alone to talk softly as they ate. She went to the den where J.D. was on the phone.

He hung it up and looked at her. "What?"

"Nothing. I thought I'd see if everything went okay with the arrangements…and give them some privacy in the kitchen as they ate their cake."

"Hey, I didn't get to finish mine."

"It's still there waiting on you. But they… This is so hard on them."

"Yeah. They like to be together. That's a good sign for two people about to get married, isn't it?" he asked with a crooked grin.

"Yes, a very good sign." Unlike them, she thought. They couldn't spend any time together without sparking off each other, sending one of them off angry or hurt. Good thing it wasn't them getting married, she thought.

She cleared her throat. "I hear hip replacements heal very quickly. Madge said her sister would only be in the hospital two or three days after surgery, as long as she had someone there to care for her. She was crying."

"She knew about the wedding. But who else are you going to call but your sister?"

"I know. I'm so glad I have two sisters now."

"Yeah, I'll bet you are." He gave her a grin and Rachel couldn't help thinking how handsome he looked when he smiled. "Could you dig me up some brothers?"

She smiled back at him. Before either of them could say anything else, Madge called to them. They returned to the kitchen.

"J.D., I need to go to a cash machine or get an advance on my salary. Taxis cost a lot and then I'll need to grocery shop and things."

"I've got cash here in the safe, Madge. How much do you think you'll need?"

"Two hundred?" Madge asked cautiously.

"I'll get it for you." He got up from the table and disappeared.

"I didn't know J.D. had a safe here," Rachel said in surprise.

"His parents had it put in. Sometimes you need cash, and his mother had some nice pieces of jewelry, things like that."

J.D. came back into the room carrying a white envelope. "I put in a little extra in case you need something you haven't thought of. I can wire you more if it's not enough."

"Can we consider it an advance on my next check?" she asked with concern in her voice.

J.D. leaned over and kissed her cheek. "Of course. I know where you live, so I'm not worried," he said, using a tough-guy accent that drew a smile from Bluey.

Madge hardly seemed to notice. She was busy counting the money. Then she stared at J.D. in shock. "J.D., you put five hundred dollars in here!"

"If you don't use it, Madge, you can always return it. I don't want you worrying about money. You'll have enough to worry about with your sister."

Madge stood up and hugged him. "You are so good to me, J.D."

Bluey shook his hand. "Thanks, J.D."

"I'm almost packed. Bluey, could you come help me finish?" Madge asked, wiping tears from her eyes.

The two disappeared.

Rachel said, "That was very good of you, J.D."

"Hell, Rachel, it's only money. Madge has done so much for me. That's nothing."

"I agree. But some men value money more than the important stuff. I'm glad to see you're not one of them."

"Those men are crazy. Or they haven't lost people they love."

They looked at each other in complete understanding. She suddenly realized that this was one of those pure moments when your soul makes a connection with another. But it was J.D....

See, said a voice inside her head, *you are right for each other, just like Madge and Bluey.*

Rachel forced her gaze away, afraid J.D. could see right through her eyes.

"I'll start dinner. Oh! I guess Madge won't be here for it. It'll just be the three of us."

"Yeah. Rachel, do I need to ask Bluey to start sleeping up here again?"

She hadn't followed his thought process. "Why would you do that?" she asked, puzzled.

"Does it bother you that it will just be the two of us at night? I can easily ask—"

"No, J.D., it doesn't bother me. I trust you."

He gave her a crooked smile. "Thanks, I think." Then he left the kitchen. His chocolate cake was still unfinished.

RACHEL TIMED DINNER to be ready when Bluey returned.

"I figured you two would've already eaten," the cowboy said when he saw the waiting meal.

"And left you with no dinner? Madge would never forgive me." Rachel gave him a grin.

When J.D. joined them, they sat down to eat. They had just gotten past the blessing and started passing the dishes when J.D. said, "Bluey, I need to ask you to sleep in the house while Madge is gone."

What? Rachel jerked her head up, staring at J.D. Just hours ago they'd decided that was unnecessary. He'd asked her opinion—which apparently he'd ignored. Her eyes, she knew, shot flares at him, but J.D. avoided her gaze.

"Well, I could, but— Oh, oh, sure, I can do that." He nodded as J.D.'s unspoken intentions became clear.

"Good," J.D. said. Then abruptly he grabbed the bowl in front of him. "Potatoes, Rachel?"

She took the dish he offered without comment. She didn't know why he'd changed his mind, unless it was because he was afraid of what people would say. Or maybe he was afraid she'd seduce him. Well, he could dream!

She kept her head down the rest of the meal, contributing nothing to the conversation.

When the meal was over, both men tried to help her with the dishes. "No, thank you. I'd rather do them alone," she insisted in cold tones.

Bluey gave her a funny look, but saying good-night, he went to the bedroom he'd been using.

"What's wrong?" J.D. asked.

Rachel didn't answer; she kept her back to him.

His big hands settled on her shoulders and he turned her to face him. "Rachel, don't try to pretend there's nothing wrong. Your body is shouting even if your voice isn't."

"You think you can read me so well?"

"Yeah, I think I can. What did I do to upset you?"

"Why did you change your mind and ask Bluey to stay?"

"Rachel—"

"I promise I won't try to seduce you!"

J.D. gave a harsh laugh. "You think I'm worried about that?" he asked, staring at her. "Damn it, Rachel, I'm worried about seducing *you,* or at least trying to. Surely you realize how much I'm attracted to you?"

What did he just say? She didn't speak, just stared at him. He'd done a hell of a job avoiding her, limiting their time together. Why, if he was as attracted to her as she was to him?

He groaned. "That's why I can't stay here alone with you. When you look at me like that, I'm ready to throw you over my shoulder and find the nearest bed."

Rachel's breathing stopped, and hope filled her heart…until J.D. spoke again.

"And that's why we need Bluey here. Because we both know that can't happen."

FOR SEVERAL DAYS, they followed a set pattern. Rachel did the chores in the house and J.D. and Bluey did the outside jobs. Once or twice, she slipped out to the barn to visit with Boomer, but other than that, she confined herself to the house.

J.D. surprised her by coming in for lunch on the third day.

"J.D.! I didn't expect you. I'll fix you a sandwich, if that's all right."

"That would be great, Rachel. Then I wondered if you'd like to go for a ride this afternoon."

Rachel's face lit up with enthusiasm. "I'd love to. It's all right if I ride by myself?"

"No, it's not all right. I thought I'd ride with you."

J.D. was actually looking to spend time with her? What about his conviction to stay clear of her, lest he be overcome by his libido? But her enthusiasm outweighed her sarcasm. She missed riding and was eager to take to her horse again. "Are you sure you can take the time off?" Rachel asked anxiously.

"I'm sure. You've certainly taken time from your schedule for us, as Bluey reminded me today. Besides, I don't want to overdo the work thing after being sick."

Rachel stared at him with confused emotions. She was upset that it had taken Bluey reminding him that he might owe her something, but she was concerned that J.D. might be feeling sick again.

"Do you not feel well? Are you running a fever?" she asked.

"I feel fine, Rachel. I was just making an excuse so you wouldn't worry about me taking time off."

"Oh. Well, I'd love to go riding," she said, smiling.

"Good. You do still have your boots and hat, don't you? I haven't seen them lately."

"I don't need either of them to cook and do laundry. I'll get them." Rachel raced to her bedroom and dragged her boots out of the back of her closet. It felt good to wear them again. She added a sweater to the short-sleeved shirt, in case it was cool out. Then she grabbed Madge's hat and hurried back to the kitchen. "I'm ready," she announced breathlessly.

"I didn't realize you missed it so much," J.D. said, frowning. "I should've done something about it before now."

"Life's been a little hectic lately."

"I've noticed that. I couldn't decide if it was because I was running at half speed or there was a lot going on."

"I think there's been a lot going on."

He held open the door for her. "By the way, it's a good thing you warned me about what you said to Stacy. From what I hear now, she's passing it around the neighborhood."

Rachel felt guilty. "I'm sorry, J.D."

"Hell, Rachel, it makes me look good, that a model has any interest in me. I'm not setting them straight."

"Being the kind of model I am isn't that big a deal," she said with a sigh.

"I don't think you'll convince any of these cowboys of that. They're all half in love with you already."

Too bad he didn't count himself in that group, Rachel thought sadly. "We're not going to rehash that, are we? I don't want you to accuse me of flirting with them again!"

They reached the barn. He grabbed her arm as they entered. "Oh, I'll beg forgiveness for that. It was Tony's fault, not yours."

"What convinced you of that?" she asked coolly.

J.D. gave a sheepish grin. "One of the other cowboys told me what an idiot he was, trying to do your job instead of his—just so he could be close to you."

"Thank you for the apology," she said quietly, and hurried out to the corral. She wasn't sure Rocky would be there.

"I brought her in on my way to the house," J.D. said as he followed her. "I figured you'd want her again."

"Oh, yes, we're great friends."

She got Rocky's bridle and climbed over the corral fence to put it on the horse. J.D. watched her, not saying anything.

"You did a good job with that," he said after she tied Rocky's reins to the rail.

"I had a good teacher."

"Yeah, I guess I did teach you that."

"Actually, I meant Billy," she said, a teasing grin on her lips.

"You'll pay for that one, Rachel," J.D. warned her.

"Ooh, I'm scared."

"Watch it, or I'll make you carry your own saddle."

"Billy taught me how to use my hip to manage the weight."

"Even so, I'll carry it for you."

After that start, their ride turned out to be perfection, in Rachel's opinion. J.D. showed her some of his favorite places on the ranch, telling her stories about his childhood. It reminded her all over again about the differences between them. Her childhood hadn't been a happy one, while he had so many happy memories of his parents.

They returned in time for her to cook a quick meal of hamburgers. As they were ready to eat, Bluey made an entrance.

J.D. greeted his cowboy and friend. "Have you talked to Madge tonight?"

"I called her just before I came in here. And thanks again, J.D., for giving me free rein of your phone. I think the calls help Madge. Her sister is doing pretty well, but she's just been out of the hospital twenty-four hours. Madge said the first few hours were tough. Her sister can be pretty grouchy."

Rachel laughed. "She can't be worse than J.D. when he's sick."

"Me? I was a perfect angel," he protested.

"Right. I should've recorded you with a video camera."

"I'll have to admit you were a might grumpier than Madge," Bluey added. "Now, she was an angel."

"Yeah, a lot of support I get from you!" J.D. chided.

"Don't pick on Bluey," Rachel said.

"What's for dessert?" J.D. asked, changing the subject abruptly.

"There's no dessert. Someone invited me for a ride. I didn't have time to make any." With her eyes she dared him to protest.

"I thought we still had some of that peach cobbler in the freezer," Bluey said.

"Shh, I was saving that for you and me," Rachel said in a mock whisper.

"Aha! I'll get it." J.D. leaped to his feet.

An hour later, dinner was over and the kitchen clean.

Bluey and J.D. were playing a game of chess in the den and Rachel had decided to indulge in a bubble bath, just to make sure she wasn't sore from riding. She'd just gotten out of the tub and into a nightgown when she heard J.D. madly swearing like she'd never heard before.

She grabbed a robe and hurried out into the kitchen. He was standing at the back door.

"J.D., what's wrong?"

He spun around and stared at her. "Why aren't you dressed?" he demanded harshly.

She blinked several times. An hour ago he'd been so sweet and lighthearted; now he resembled a bear without honey. "Because I just got out of the bathtub," she replied.

"Damn it, go away."

She took a step back. "Do you mean go to bed, or go pack my bags?"

"No, I don't mean pack your bags. I've done everything I can to protect you from me, but now Bluey's gone, probably for the night."

"Where did he go?"

"Tony bought an expensive horse. It's sick and the vet is out on another call. Bluey's our best man with sick animals, so Tony asked him to come sit up with him and tend his horse."

"That's very good of Bluey."

"Yeah, real great."

"I still don't understand what you're upset about."

J.D. walked toward her, a dark, fiery look in his eyes that had her backing up another couple of steps.

"Rachel, the only thing that will keep me from taking you to bed is if you say no. I've resisted you as long and as hard as I can. But if you don't say no right now, it's going to happen. I'm going to throw you over my shoulder and head for my bedroom."

Chapter Sixteen

J.D. stood there waiting for the no he expected to hear.

Rachel said nothing.

"Didn't you hear me, Rachel? Tell me no!"

In a whisper, she said, "Is that what you want?"

"What I want doesn't matter! It's what you want that's important." He watched her closely, his heart thumping in his chest.

"I can't."

J.D. hung his head. He'd known she wouldn't be interested in him. He turned around, planning on walking around the house fifty times in the night air. That might curb his urges. Yeah, right.

"I can't say no," Rachel explained.

J.D.'s head snapped up. "What are you saying?"

"Do I have to draw you a road map, J.D.? I'm saying yes…if you want me."

"Damn it, Rachel, I'm going crazy with wanting you. I have been ever since we were together during the shoot. But I'm trying to be fair. You're the one in control here. You don't have to do anything you don't want to do."

"I haven't stopped wanting you since then, either," she said, taking a step toward him.

He crossed the distance between them in no time and took her in his arms. "Why didn't you tell me?"

"A woman doesn't like to beg."

"Neither does a man," he told her just before his lips took hers. After several deep, probing kisses, he did as he'd promised and swung her up into his arms. "Last chance, Rachel."

"I know. Hurry up."

When they reached his bedroom, he set her feet on the floor and kissed her again. "I've dreamed of having you here for so long, it's hard to believe it's true."

"Want me to convince you?" she asked, emboldened by his honesty. With her gaze fixed on him, she removed her robe. His eyes widened and his nostrils flared.

Rachel was encouraged by his reaction. She pulled her nightgown over her head, leaving only her panties to cover her.

"Mercy, Rachel, you're driving me crazy," he said, breathing heavily as he wrapped his arms around her warm body.

"You're wearing too many clothes, J.D. I feel like I'm the only one who's working at this."

He immediately ripped his shirt free of his jeans. She began helping him unbutton it. J.D. abandoned that task to her and undid his jeans. They fell around his feet but didn't come off. He'd forgotten to remove his boots.

"My boots! I've got to get my boots off!"

Rachel began to laugh.

J.D. stared at her. "What's so funny?"

"In my dreams, our clothes magically disappeared. Reality is a little different, isn't it?"

"Your clothes disappeared fast enough," J.D. told her. "For which I'm grateful. But I'll try to do better."

"I'm not complaining, J.D. The view is spectacular." She sat down on the bed, watching him.

He sat down beside her and kissed her. "Now I'm going to remove my boots. Don't go anywhere."

"I won't," Rachel said, drawing in a deep breath. She ran a hand up his back as he leaned forward to tug on his footwear.

He straightened up and took her in his arms, kissing her desperately. Then he said, "Don't touch me until I get these damn boots off, Rachel, or I'm going to explode." He started working on his boots again.

Rachel was tempted to ignore his request. His broad shoulders gleamed in the light and his muscled back offered a wide expanse of warm skin. She drew another deep breath, trying to calm down.

He sat up and stared at her. "You okay?"

"Yes. Can I touch now?"

"I'm all yours, Rachel," he told her as he lay down on the bed and pulled her with him.

Wrapped in his arms, Rachel felt the same thrill of excitement as she had last time, only now she knew him so well, so much better than she had before, which only enhanced their physical closeness. She ran her hands over his muscular chest. "You'd think you were a weight lifter," she said.

"I am. I lift bales of hay," he said with a chuckle.

"My dad always said working hard was better than working out."

"I couldn't agree more," she said, pressing her lips to his chest.

He returned the favor, cupping her breasts and kissing them. Then he ran his hands down her body. "Rachel, you drive me crazy with wanting you."

"You do have a condom, don't you?" she whispered urgently, realizing neither of them was going to last much longer.

"I've been stockpiling them for months, praying I'd get another chance," he whispered in return, reaching over her to his bedside table. He opened a drawer and pulled out the necessary item.

He slid his briefs down and kicked them off. Then he attended to Rachel's panties. Soon they were skin to skin, sharing their heat and their passion.

Haunted by memories, they raced to replace them with even better ones. J.D. made love to every inch of her and Rachel returned the favor. She loved this man, both inside and out. Whatever happened in the future, she wanted this moment in time and she held nothing back.

As he entered her, her name was on J.D.'s lips. He called it out as if it was a plea. For what, he didn't know. He already had everything he wanted. He had Rachel.

Then it hit him. He wanted forever.

When their frantic passion was sated, they lay in each other's arms, their shallow breathing gradually deepening. J.D. couldn't let her go, even though he could scarcely move.

Rachel snuggled closer, and he bent down and

pulled the covers over them. Their eyes gradually closed as their bodies relaxed.

An hour later, J.D. awakened, savoring the feel of Rachel next to him. He couldn't resist running his hands over her smooth body. When she responded, the guilt he felt at waking her disappeared.

They again made love, this time slowly, exploring each other's body. J.D. discovered Rachel was ticklish, something he loved.

"J.D.," Rachel warned, scooting away. "I'm not coming close if you're going to tickle me."

"Hey, I promise I won't, 'cause I want you close," he agreed with a chuckle. "I just didn't expect it."

"It's not something I mention to strangers," she said huffily.

"I'm not exactly a stranger, sweetheart. But don't worry. I won't tell anyone." He kissed her, hoping to take her mind off her weakness. It made her prickly.

She wrapped her arms around his neck and pressed closer, which was exactly what he wanted.

This time, after the passion subsided, J.D. intended to talk, to express what he was feeling. But the lovemaking was too intense, too demanding, and they both fell asleep.

When the alarm went off the next morning, at six o'clock, J.D. wearily reached to turn it off. As tempted as he was to ignore the demands of his life, he knew he couldn't. He looked at the beautiful woman in his bed, determined not to mess up this time.

"Rachel," he whispered, gently shaking her shoulder.

Slowly her eyes opened and she stared up at him. "What?"

"I have to get up now. I'll make you a deal."

"What deal?" she asked groggily.

"You can sleep in this morning and I'll make my own breakfast, if you'll agree to one thing."

"Okay. What?"

"Be here when I get home."

She relaxed against the pillows. "Not a problem. It's where I want to be."

"Good," he said, leaning over to kiss her thoroughly, hoping she wouldn't forget it. Then he got out of bed. "I'll see you tonight."

He quietly dressed as she slept, his gaze traveling over her body under the covers. Every inch of her pleased him. He was so grateful for getting a second chance with Rachel.

He headed to the kitchen for a quick breakfast before he saddled up.

RACHEL WOKE A LITTLE after nine. Since she usually got up at six, she felt sinfully lazy, but she loved it. Stretching beneath the covers, she savored each memory they'd made last night.

Finally, with a yawn, she got out of bed. Returning to her room, she showered and dressed. Then she headed to the kitchen, her stomach growling.

After breakfast, she made the bed and put in a load of laundry. Then she debated what to do next. She had some chores waiting, but she wanted to bake something. Something J.D. liked. She was looking through Madge's cookbook when the phone rang.

"Hello?"

"Rachel! It's Rebecca. Vivian's gone into labor. They've taken her to the hospital."

"Slow down, Becca. What does the doctor say?"

"You know doctors. They don't tell you anything until after the fact! She's so early…. Oh, Rachel, I wish you were here. Vanessa and I need you."

Rachel figured part of Rebecca's emotional response was because of her own pregnancy, but that was all the more reason to comfort her.

"I'm coming, honey. I'll be there in three hours. Will you be at the hospital?"

"Yes. Peter is going to pick up Joey and take him to Vivian's for Betty to watch him. I'm picking up Vanessa and we're going straight to the hospital. Will is already there, of course. Oh, Rachel, I'm so glad you're coming."

"I'm glad you called. I'm on my way."

She grabbed the walkie-talkie. "Base to J.D. Come in, please."

Nothing happened.

Was he in a low spot where he couldn't receive the message? She'd try again later. Packing an overnight bag was what she should do now.

That didn't take long.

She found Madge's keys and placed them on the table by her overnight bag. Then she grabbed the walkie-talkie again. "Base to J.D. Come in, please."

Still nothing. What was she going to do? She couldn't leave without letting him know why.

She grabbed a piece of paper and a pen and quickly wrote a note explaining her disappearance. J.D. would understand. He'd already shown her that family was important. She left the note on the table. Then she grabbed her purse, keys and bag and ran outside to Madge's car.

J.D. RODE TOWARD THE BARN, anticipation rising in him. He'd decided to come in for lunch and surprise Rachel.

Striding to the house, he looked forward to the pleasure he'd see on her face. They'd crossed some invisible barrier last night. He knew she loved him. Now he had to say the words to her, verbally commit to her, and he was ready. More than ready.

He bounded into the house, a big smile on his face. But it faded when he found the house empty. He knew it almost at once. Racing through the kitchen to his bedroom, he found the bed neatly made, as if the pleasure they'd shared there had been erased.

He went to Rachel's room next. Empty.

It couldn't have happened again. She couldn't have walked out on him, leaving no word, no promises, no future.

Slowly, he walked back into the kitchen.

No Rachel.

He fell into a chair at the table and put his head down on his arms. He couldn't believe it. Last night, and this morning, she'd been so loving, so responsive to his lovemaking.

He wearily raised his head. Out of the corner of his eye, he caught some movement, and looked beneath the table to see a piece of paper fluttering in the breeze he'd created as he moved.

His heart beat faster as he reached for it. Immediately he saw Rachel's writing. It was difficult to concentrate enough to read. She hadn't left without a word.

She'd left a note, signed "Love, Rachel."

Then the message penetrated his exultant brain. Vivian was in labor. Her sisters needed her at the hospital. She'd be back as soon as she could.

J.D. got up and looked out the window. Madge's car was gone. He checked his watch. Then he looked back at the note. She'd jotted down the time she'd left—two hours earlier.

He called the airport and asked for a plane to fly him to Dallas, just as he had for Madge. Then he grabbed the walkie-talkie. He knew at once it wasn't working. The battery must be low. But he wasn't going to let that stop him. He went to the bunkhouse and told Cook to tell Bluey he was in charge and to give him Rachel's note. He'd understand why J.D. had to go.

Then he packed a few items for a couple of nights and jumped in his truck. He didn't have much time before he'd be in the air on his way to Rachel.

She might not have walked away on purpose this time, but he wasn't taking any chances.

RACHEL FOLLOWED DIRECTIONS to the maternity waiting room, moving quickly down the long hospital corridors. She stepped into the room, her gaze searching for her sisters. They were sitting together, talking quietly, holding hands, their faces tense with worry.

"Rachel!" Vanessa exclaimed, jumping up when she saw her.

Rebecca was only seconds behind her younger sister, slowed slightly by her pregnancy. They exchanged a group hug that was fierce with love.

"Oh, we're so glad you're here," Rebecca whispered.

"What's happening? Have the doctors said anything?"

"No," Vanessa said. "Will's come out a couple of times to reassure us, but he's worried. You can see it on his face."

"Where's Jeff?"

"He's coming," Rebecca said. "He was in court in Fort Worth, with his phone turned off when I tried to call him. I left a message and he called me back about half an hour ago, so he should be here soon." Rebecca drew a deep breath to calm herself. Then she took a close look at her twin. "Rachel, you look good. How do you feel?"

"Wonderful. I've learned to cook, Rebecca, and I can ride a horse, too. I love living on the ranch."

Vanessa and Rebecca exchanged another worried look, then Vanessa said, "But it's only temporary, Rachel. Isn't it?"

Instead of Rachel answering, a strong masculine voice responded. "No, it's not temporary. It's forever, if she wants it to be."

Rachel jumped up and spun around to look J.D. Stanley in the eye. "J.D.!" she exclaimed, and fell into his open arms. "Yes, J.D., I want it to be permanent. I'm so glad you came."

"I wasn't about to be left behind, sweetheart. I made that mistake last time. It won't happen again." He kissed her, a promise underscored.

"Wow!" Vanessa said, watching them.

Rebecca was beaming. "Oh, Rachel, I'm so happy for you."

Leaning against J.D., her head on his shoulder, Rachel was the epitome of contentment. Then she straightened. "How did you get here so quickly? I tried the walkie-talkie and you didn't answer."

"I tried it, too. I think it needs new batteries. But I came in for lunch and got your note. I didn't want to waste any time so I flew up. Which means I can drive back with you."

"Perfect," Rachel said, smiling.

"Becca?" Jeff called as he came in the room.

Rebecca rushed over, eager to be enclosed in her husband's embrace. "Oh, Jeff, I'm so glad you're here."

"Sorry it took so long, sweetheart," he told her, not letting her go.

She nodded over her shoulder to Rachel and J.D. "Oh, honey, have you met J.D.? And Rachel's back. Doesn't she look good?"

"Yeah." Jeff released his wife and led her across the room. Sticking out his right hand, he said, "J.D., I'm Jeff Jacobs. How are you?"

"Jeff, I'm glad to meet you."

They each had an arm around a twin. Jeff looked at J.D. and Rachel and said, "You're looking good, Rachel. Do you have an announcement to make?"

J.D. didn't wait for her to say anything. "We're getting married," he answered proudly.

"Welcome to the family," Jeff said with a grin. "It's a great one."

"I agree."

"When are you marrying?" Vanessa asked.

Rachel and J.D. looked at each other.

She spoke first. "I'd like to share our wedding with Madge and Bluey, just like we planned."

"You already planned to marry?" Rebecca asked, surprised.

"No. We were planning *their* wedding. I think it would be nice to share it, if they don't mind." She looked at J.D. again, a question in her eyes.

"I think they'll love the idea."

"So, when will that be?" Rebecca asked, wanting a date.

"We don't know yet. Madge's sister broke her hip and we had to postpone the wedding. But it should be soon."

"It had better be soon," J.D. growled, pulling her into his arms again. When he kissed her, Rachel could feel his eagerness. It matched her own. She gave herself over to the kiss, ignoring the onlookers in the waiting room.

They stopped being the center of attention when Will Greenfield, Vivian's husband, burst into the room. He was wearing a pair of scrubs and on the front of his shirt were two tiny, freshly made footprints.

"He's here! We've got our son! He's perfect. And Vivian is doing great. I'm so proud of her." Will was practically shouting, he was so excited. All the young women hugged him, but they were careful not to mess up the footprints. The two men shook his hand.

Then Will must have realized J.D. was there. "Did you bring Rachel? If so, we appreciate it."

J.D. laughed. "No, I didn't bring Rachel. I followed her. I wasn't about to let her get away." As if to underscore his words, he put his arm around her and pulled her against him. "We're getting married."

Will shook his hand. "May I tell Vivian? She'll be so pleased. She's been worrying about Rachel."

J.D. looked down at her. "Is that okay with you, honey, if Will tells Vivian?"

Rachel stepped forward and hugged Will again. "Of course you can tell her. I would've let her know earlier, but J.D. didn't mention marriage until we got here."

Will raised an eyebrow at J.D., who actually blushed.

"I was thinking it all along, but I wasn't sure of Rachel until…recently," he finished awkwardly.

Will laughed. "I understand perfectly."

THREE WEEKS LATER, on a beautiful spring Sunday afternoon, a wedding occurred on J.D.'s ranch.

All of Rachel's family was in attendance, which now included Daniel William Greenfield, three weeks old and usually the center of attention. Today, he was outranked by two blushing brides.

Madge was dressed in a stylish pale blue suit and a small hat with an attached veil. She carried a beautiful bouquet of spring flowers.

Rachel was wearing Rebecca's wedding dress and veil. It was a perfect fit and complemented her dark hair. She loved wearing her twin's gown, feeling as if it connected her to her newfound family. As she walked down the aisle Vanessa leaned over and whispered to

Rebecca, "Save this dress for me, okay, sis? I think it has magic powers."

"That's a deal. Do you have an eye on someone?"

"Nope, but it's nice to know the dress is waiting."

They shared a smile before Rachel continued to walk toward J.D.

Rachel had decided against having bridesmaids. She'd suggested that she and Madge walk down the "aisle" together, toward a trellis with interwoven ivy and white carnations. When they reached the altar, she and J.D. acted as attendants to Bluey and Madge, and then they changed places, with Bluey and Madge serving as their attendants.

After the beautiful ceremony, the couples led their guests—consisting of the entire neighborhood, Rachel's family and Madge's sister, who was moving extremely well—to a table where two majestic cakes awaited them.

Rachel and Madge each cut the first piece of her cake and fed a bite to her new husband, then vice versa. Rebecca and Vanessa continued cutting cake for their guests.

The two couples moved through the crowd, welcoming their friends and family. Little Danny received a lot of attention, which, of course, pleased his doting parents. Joey liked his new family member, but told his aunt Rachel that he wasn't that great. He couldn't even play ball yet! Joey was much more interested in the horses he could see in the distance on J.D.'s ranch.

After the cake had been served, Rebecca sat down next to her twin. "I never thought I'd see you living on a ranch, happy to be a cowgirl."

"But I'm happy, Becca."

Rebecca grinned. "I can see that. And J.D. seems to be a good man."

"Yes, I think so." The smile that had adorned Rachel's face for weeks suddenly faded as she said, "It's too bad Jim couldn't have been here. I told you his leave got canceled, didn't I?"

"Yeah. And no wonder. Things aren't going smoothly over there."

"I know. I'll be glad when he's home."

Vanessa joined them, taking a seat and putting her feet up. "Everything's going well, isn't it?"

"I think so," Rebecca said. "We were just talking about Jim."

"I know. The news isn't so good. Will's still working on finding David. Maybe he'll turn up soon."

"I hope so," Rachel said. "I'd love for us all to be together someday."

"And speaking of togetherness…" J.D. swooped in and grabbed her. He drew her apart from their guests for a moment of togetherness. "Rachel, you're so beautiful!"

"You know that's not what matters," she chided gently.

He laughed and added, "I meant on the inside, of course."

They both laughed. Then Rachel gave a sigh of satisfaction. "You asked for some brothers, didn't you? I've managed to give you one, in Jeff, and maybe, if Will finds David and Jim comes home, you'll have two more."

"True. Or Vanessa may marry."

"Have you heard something? She hasn't mentioned anyone."

"I've just noticed the cowboys circling her. She draws attention, because she looks so much like her big sisters, and they're beautiful…on the inside." Then he kissed her before she could say anything.

"Rachel, I'm the luckiest man in the world. I'm sorry we can't go on our honeymoon at once."

"It's all right. It's like Bluey said. They don't have as much time as we do. We'll manage just fine here."

"I hope we have a century of being together," he whispered.

She faced him. "However long we have, we're lucky to have found each other again. Don't ever let me go, J.D. I'd be lost without you."

"Never, my love. You're mine forever. And I'm yours."

* * * * *

And don't miss
A SOLDIER'S RETURN
by Judy Christenberry
The next captivating episode
of the beloved family saga

THE CHILDREN OF TEXAS

Separated during childhood, the Barlow family is des-
tined to rediscover one another and find true love in the
Lone Star State. Catch the next emotion-filled reunion
in which the Barlow sisters are reunited with their long-
lost big brother....

In
A SOLDIER'S RETURN
by Judy Christenberry
Coming only to Harlequin American Romance
In July 2005

Welcome to the world of American Romance!
Turn the page for excerpts
from our April 2005 titles.

SPRING IN THE VALLEY by Charlotte Douglas

DISCOVERING DUNCAN by Mary Anne Wilson

MAD ABOUT MAX by Penny McCusker

LOVE, TEXAS by Ginger Chambers

We're sure you'll enjoy every one of these books!

Spring in the Valley (#1061) is the third book in Charlotte Douglas's popular series A PLACE TO CALL HOME. The previous titles are *Almost Heaven* and *One Good Man*.

When you read *Spring in the Valley,* you'll meet local police officer Brynn Sawyer and New York City attorney Rand Benedict, who's come to Pleasant Valley with his orphaned nephew. Brynn and Rand quickly develop a relationship—but Rand has a secret agenda that's going to affect not only Brynn but the whole town. Still, Rand will find himself enchanted by Pleasant Valley.... It's the kind of place where neighbors become friends and where people care—small-town life as it was meant to be!

Hiking her long silk skirt above her boots, Officer Brynn Sawyer slid from the car and used her Mag-Lite to guide her steps to the idling Jaguar she'd pulled over. At her approach, the driver's window slid down with an electronic whir.

The driver started to speak. "I have a—"

"I'll do the talking. This is a state highway, not a NASCAR track," Brynn said in the authoritative manner she reserved for lawbreakers, especially those displaying such an obvious lack of common sense. "And the road's icing up. You have a death wish?"

"No." The driver seemed distracted, oblivious to the seriousness of his offense. "I need to—"

"Turn off your engine," Brynn ordered, "and place your hands on the wheel where I can see them."

She shined her flashlight in the driver's face. The man, who was in his mid-thirties, squinted in the brightness, but not before the pupils of his eyes, the color of dark melting chocolate, contracted in the light. She instantly noted the rugged angle of his unshaven jaw, the aristocratic nose, baby-fine brown hair tousled as if he'd just climbed out of bed...

And a wad of one-hundred-dollar bills thrust under her nose.

Anger burned through her, but she kept her temper. "If that's a bribe, buster, you're in a heap of trouble."

"No bribe." His tone, although frantic, was rich and full. "Payment for my fine. I can't stop—"

"You can't keep going at your previous speed either," she said reasonably and struggled to control her fury at the man's arrogance. "You'll kill yourself and someone else—"

"It's Jared. I have to get him to the hospital."

Labored breathing sounded in the back seat. Brynn aimed her light at the source. In a child carrier, a tow-headed toddler, damp hair matted to his head and plump cheeks flushed with fever, wheezed violently as his tiny chest struggled for air.

Brynn's anger vanished at the sight of the poor little guy, and her sympathy kicked in. She made a quick decision.

"Follow me. I'll radio ahead for the E.R. to expect us."

With *Discovering Duncan* (#1062), Mary Anne Wilson launches a brand-new four-book series, RETURN TO SILVER CREEK. In these stories, various characters return to a Nevada town for a variety of reasons— to hide, to come home, to confront their pasts. In *Discovering Duncan,* a young private detective, Lauren Carter, is hired to track down a wealthy client's son. When she does so, she also discovers the person he really is—not to mention the delights of this small mountain town!

"I'm a man of patience," D. R. Bishop said as his secretary left, closing the door securely behind her. "But even I have my limits."

Lauren Carter never took her eyes off the large man across from her at the impressive stone and glass desk. D. R. Bishop was dressed all in black. He was a huge, imposing man, and definitely, despite what he said, a man with little patience. He looked tightly wound, and ready to spring.

Lauren sat very still in a terribly uncomfortable chair, her hands in her lap while she let D. R. Bishop do all the talking. She simply nodded from time to time.

"My son walked out on everything six months ago," he said.

"Why?"

He tented his fingers thoughtfully, with his elbows resting on the polished desktop, as if he were considering her single-word question. But she knew he was considering just how much to tell her. His eyes were dark as night, a contrast to his snow-white hair and meticulously trimmed beard. "Ah, that's a good question," he said. For some reason, he was hedging.

"Mr. Bishop, you've dealt with the Sutton Agency enough to know that privacy and discretion are part of our service. Nothing you tell me will go any farther."

He shrugged his massive shoulders and sank back in his chair. "Of course. I expect no less," he said.

"So, why did your son leave?"

"I thought it was a middle-age crisis of some sort." He smiled slightly, a strained expression. "Not that thirty-eight is middle-aged. Then I thought he might be having a breakdown. Maybe gone over the edge." The man stood abruptly, rising to his full, imposing height, and she could've sworn she felt the air ripple around her from his movement. "But he's not crazy, Ms. Carter, he's just damn stubborn. Too damn stubborn."

She waited as he walked to the windows behind him and faced the city twenty floors below. When he didn't speak, she finally said, "You don't know why he left?"

The shoulders shrugged again. "A difference of opinion on how to do business. Nothing new for us." He spoke without turning. "We've always clashed, but in the end, we've always managed to make our business relationship work."

"What exactly do you want from the Sutton Agency, Mr. Bishop?"

"Find him."

"That's it?"

He turned back to her, studying her intently for several moments before he said, "No."

"Then what else do you want us to do?"

"As an employee of Sutton, I want you to find my son. I also want him to come back willingly."

"Okay," she said. She'd handle it. She had to. Her future depended on finding the mysterious Duncan Bishop.

We're thrilled to introduce a brand-new writer to American Romance! *Mad About Max* (#1063) is the first of three books by Penny McCusker. They're set in Erskine, Montana, where the residents gather at the Ersk Inn to trade gossip and place bets in the watering hole's infamous betting pools. Cute, klutzy schoolteacher Sara Lewis is the current subject of one of the inn's most popular pools ever. She's been secretly (or not so secretly!) pining for rancher and single dad Max Devlin for going on six years, and this story sees her about to take her destiny into her own hands.

Penny writes with the perfect mix of warmth and humor, and her characters will have you cheering for them right to the end.

"Please tell me that wasn't Super Glue."

Sara Lewis tore her gaze away from the gorgeous— and worried—blue eyes of Max Devlin, looking up to where her hands were flattened against the wall over his head. Even when she saw the damning evidence squished between her right palm and her third-grade class's mangled Open House banner, she refused to admit it, even to herself.

If she admitted she was holding a drained tube of Super Glue in her hand, she might begin to wonder if there'd been any stray drops. And where they might have landed. That sort of speculation would only lead her to conclusions she'd be better off not drawing, conclusions like there was no way a stray drop could have landed on the floor. Not with her body plastered to Max's. No, that kind of speculation would lead her right into trouble.

As if she could have gotten into any more trouble.

She'd been standing on a chair, putting up the banner her third-grade class had created to welcome their parents to Erskine Elementary's Open House. But her hands had jerked when she heard Max's voice out in the hallway, and she'd torn it clear in half. She'd grabbed the first thing off her desk that might save the irreplaceable strip of laboriously scrawled greetings and brilliant artwork and jumped back on her chair, only to find that Max had gotten there first. He'd grabbed one end of the banner, then dived for the other as it fluttered away, ending up spread-eagled against the wall, one end of the banner in either hand, trapped there by Sara and her chair.

She'd pulled the ragged ends of the banner together, but just as she'd started to glue them, Max had turned around and nearly knocked her over. "Hold still," she'd said sharply, not quite allowing herself to notice that he was facing her now, that perfect male body against hers, that heart-stopping face only inches away. Instead, she'd asked him to hold the banner in place while she applied the glue. The rest was history. Or in her case infamy.

"Uh, Sara..." Max was trying to slide out from between her and the wall, but she met his eyes again and shook her head.

"Uh, just hold on a little longer, Max. I want to make sure the glue is dry."

What she really needed was a moment to figure out how badly she'd humiliated herself this time. Experimentally, she stuck out her backside. Sure enough, the front of her red pleather skirt tented dead center, stuck fast to the lowermost pearl button on Max's shirt—the button that was right above his belt buckle, which was right above his—

Sara slammed her hips back against his belly, an automatic reaction intended to halt the dangerous direction of her thoughts and hide the proof of her latest misadventure. It was like throwing fuel on the fire her imagination had started.

Blood rushed into her face, then drained away to throb deep and low, just about where his belt buckle was digging into her—

"Sara!"

She snapped back to reality, noting the exasperation in his voice. Reluctantly she arched away from him. The man had to breathe, after all.

"There's a perfectly reasonable explanation for this," she said in a perfectly reasonable voice. In fact, that voice amazed her, considering that she was glued to a man she'd been secretly in love with for the better part of six years.

"There always is, Sara," Max said, exasperation giving way to amusement. "There was a perfectly reasonable explanation for how Mrs. Tilford's cat wound up on top of the church bell tower."

Sara grimaced.

"There was a perfectly reasonable explanation for why Jenny Hastings went into the Crimp 'N Cut a blonde and came out a redhead. Barn-red."

Sara cringed.

"And there was a perfectly reasonable explanation for the new stained-glass window in the town hall looking more like an advertisement for a brothel than a reenactment of Erskine's founding father rescuing the Indian maidens."

She huffed out a breath, indignant. "I only broke the one pane."

"Yeah, the pane between the grateful, kneeling maidens and the very happy Jim 'Mountain Man' Erskine."

"The talk would die down if the mayor let me get the pane fixed instead of just shoving the rest of them together so it looked like the Indian maidens were, well, really grateful."

"People are coming from miles around to see it," Max reminded her. "He'd lose the vote of every businessman in town if he ruined the best moneymaker they've ever had."

Sara just huffed out another breath. It was a little hypocritical for the people of Erskine, Montana, to pick on her for something they were capitalizing on, especially when she had a perfectly good reason for why it had happened, why bad luck seemed to follow her around like a black cloud. Except she couldn't tell anyone what that reason was, especially not Max. Because he was the reason.

Veteran author Ginger Chambers returns to American Romance with *Love, Texas,* a warm, engrossing story about returning to your past—coming home—and seeing it in an entirely new way…. You'll enjoy Ginger's determined and delightful heroine, Cassie Edwards, and her rancher hero, Will Taylor. Cassie is more and more drawn into life at the Taylor ranch—and you will be, too. Guaranteed you'll feel right at home in Love, Texas!

When Cassie Edwards arrived at the Four Corners—where Main Street was intersected by Pecan—nothing in Love, Texas, seemed to have changed. At Swanson's Garage the same old-style gasoline pumps waited for customers under the same rickety canopy. The Salon of Beauty still sported the same eye-popping candy-pink front door. Handy Grocery & Hardware's windows were plastered with what could be the same garish sale banners. And from the number of pickup trucks and cars crowded into the parking lot on the remaining corner, Reva's Café still claimed the prize as the area's most popular eating place.

Old feelings of panic threatened to engulf Cassie, forcing her to pull the car onto the side of the road. She had to remember she wasn't the same Cassie Edwards the people of Love thought they knew so well. She'd changed.

Cassie gripped the steering wheel. She'd come here to do a job—to negotiate a land deal, get the needed signatures, then get out…fast!

A flutter of unease went through her as her thoughts moved to her mother, but she quickly beat it down. She'd known all along that she'd have to see her. But the visit would be brief and it would be the last thing she did before starting back for Houston. She glanced in the rearview mirror and pulled back out onto Main and continued toward the Taylor ranch.

Cassie drove down the highway, following a line of tightly strung barbed wire that enclosed grazing Black Angus cattle. The working fence ran for about a mile before being replaced by a rustic rock fence that decorated either side of a wide metal gate, on which the ranch's name, the Circle Bar-T, was proudly displayed in a circle of black wrought-iron. A sprawling two-story white frame house with a wraparound porch sat a distance down the driveway, the rugged landscape around it softened with flowers and more delicate greenery.

Cassie hopped out of the car, swung open the gate and drove through.

"Hey!" a man shouted.

Cassie looked around and saw a jeans-clad man in a long-sleeved shirt and bone-colored hat heading toward her, and he didn't look pleased. She'd had a thing for Will Taylor when she'd first started to notice boys.

Trim and athletic with thick blond hair and eyes the same blue as the Texas sky, he was handsome in the way that made a girl's heart quicken if he so much as looked at her. But even if he had noticed her in the same way she'd noticed him, there'd been a gulf between them far wider than the difference in their ages. She was Bonnie Edwards's daughter. And that was enough.

"You forgot somethin', ma'am," he drawled. "You didn't close the gate. In these parts if you open a gate, you need to close it."

Will Taylor continued to look at her. Was he starting to remember her, too?

He broke into her thoughts. "Just go knock on the front door. My mom's expectin' you." Then, with a little nod, he stuffed his hat back on his head and walked away.

Cassie stared after him. Not exactly an auspicious beginning.

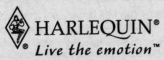

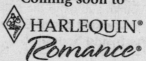
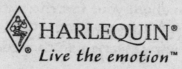

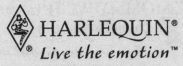